Doctor Hydenberg

Jeffery Martin Botzenhart

ALL RIGHTS RESERVED

Publisher's Note:

This is a work of fiction. All names, characters, places, and events are the work of the author's imagination.

Any resemblance to real persons, places, or events is coincidental.

Solstice Publishing -
www.solsticepublishing.com

Doctor Hydenberg
By
Jeffery Martin Botzenhart

Chapter One

"I am so looking forward to being a corpse."

Benjamin's heart sank to his stomach in hearing his only friend utter such a terrible remark. Glancing wearily at Peter, the extent of the inexplicable ailment ravaging his body proved most evident by his lifeless facial expression. Pale skin coloration and sunken eyes staring off unnerved him, as did the tremors coursing through his limbs. The shadow of whiskers and wrinkles adorning his complexion caused him to appear ever so more than their shared age of forty.

Attempting levity Benjamin wryly responded, "I have always admired your resolve to be brutally blunt."

Peter erupted with laughter until overcome by a coughing spell. Benjamin held out a crystal goblet of water but Peter waved his frail hand to refuse the offer.

"I would much prefer a hearty ale."

Motioning toward the bottles of wine on the table next to Peter's bed, Benjamin commented, "While I carry no ale with me, I could pour you a sip of one of these fine vintages."

"*French*, all of them," Peter uttered with disgust. "I would rather drink my own piss than consume even a drop from any of those bottles. I am certain Angelique or Genevieve poisoned them—and do not attempt to convince me this has failed to cross you mind. I know you too well. I do not see you drinking either."

Sighing, Benjamin confessed, "And you will not. I am beyond baffled by what has stricken you, causing your health to deteriorate so severely over such a short time. Yet as much as I regret entertaining this notion, suspicion of either of them poisoning you has crossed my mind."

"Your flawless intelligence does you credit."

"As does your rampant paranoia."

A hush fell between them. Benjamin watched Peter's eyes close for a moment and then rapidly blink.

"You should get some rest."

"I will achieve an endless amount of rest when I am dead," Peter commented. "Our time, my friend, draws to a close. You know this to be true."

Lowering his eyes, Benjamin nodded and responded, "Yes, I believe so."

"My friend, you have remained by my side, unfailing in offering your friendship, while my devil of a wife and her vile lady in waiting have driven all others away. I could not fathom facing my final hours without you."

Again in attempt to lighten the enveloping heaviness of the moment, Benjamin commented, "Well… my social engagements were rather sparse this evening."

"Bloody bastard," Peter remarked with a smile. His expression turned solemn. "Within the coming days, my final will and testament will be read, unleashing indignation from most."

"How so?"

"While my adulterous wife has been away in Paris these last two weeks, I have sold Rothschild Hall and have altered my will in bequeathing my accumulated fortune to a complete stranger."

"Who?"

"I have never met him—yet before dawn *you will*."

"I fail to understand all this," Benjamin uttered. "I agree your wife is a cunning liar and adulterous and deserves nothing less than your scorn. I am baffled, though, why you would bequeath your fortune to a man you have never met."

"There is logic behind my madness, I assure you," Peter responded. "My friend, we are both well-versed with theory and execution in games of greed. Angelique and Genevieve have proven to be skilled mistresses of such. The very day I stepped foot on Martinique proved the commencement of my financial and emotional demise as a result of this. The first moment I laid eyes on Angelique I fell under the seduction of her dark charms. She led me astray of rational convictions. I became drunk on the forbidden nectar of lust. Willingly I offered her my heart… only to have it crushed by her false whispers of love and devotion. What she desired most was fortune. It is that, my friend, which we will deny her in the end."

"Certainly she will challenge this as well as the sale of the estate?"

"Undoubtedly," Peter agreed. "Angelique will demand an inquiry—and both she and Genevieve will exploit their charms in efforts to sway opinion, attempting to prove my fragile mental state. Many a times a seemingly distraught widow has swayed court opinion in obtaining that which was not left to her by spiteful husbands, such as me. There *would* be a silver lining to such spectacle, setting a fire to the tongues of malicious gossip mongers.

My dreadful sister, Mercedes, might seek her share of the fortune as well. Such an atrocious woman she is. Her piercing stare alone could cause one to soil his undergarments. Yet, if my plan finds success, with their greed unsatisfied and fortune lost, Angelique and Genevieve will be forced out onto the streets and made to forage for scraps in dark alleys like other bitches."

Staring at his friend, Benjamin commented, "I know you well, Peter. There is a facet of your revenge against you wife and Genevieve—that you have not yet divulged."

"Correct, my dear Benjamin. This is where you—and your *remarkable* theory must now be addressed."

"Again, I fail to understand."

Peter weakly grinned before revealing, "For you, I have found the perfect host to test your theory on."

"*Peter—*."

"No, my friend," Peter interrupted. "The time for doubt has come and gone. I am *convinced* of the success you will achieve with this endeavor."

"But… as I have told you many times my research is *only* theory and conjecture," Benjamin insisted. "No practical application can be sought without the existence of—"

"A proper host," Peter again interrupted him, "one gifted and unique."

"Yes. Mark my words, though. What you seek you will not find."

"Oh, but I have, my friend, in the most unlikely of places."

"Where?"

"The Mooreland Asylum for the Criminally Insane."

Benjamin's breath rushed from his lungs as his jaw dropped. "Are… you… barking? Your intentions—are for me… to… obtain a host from an asylum for the criminally insane?"

"He is not interned there, but merely an orderly meagerly employed in the wards. His name is Heathcliff Gray."

"How can you be certain he is the one?"

"I have known for some time now."

"And—you kept this hidden from me?"

"I kept this hidden from all—until a month ago, which by *coincidence*—or *not* coincided with when I fell ill. I was careless and should have been more vigilant to the threats surrounding me."

"Who is this *Heathcliff Gray*?"

"He is my son."

Benjamin's jaw fell, astonished by this revelation.

"Twenty odd years ago I found myself in a forbidden affair with a chambermaid in the service of my parents," Peter confessed. "I loved her with all my heart and had hoped to ask her to marry me… but my parents were furious, thinking only of the scandal that would ensue, threatening our social standing. As fate would have it, this chambermaid disappeared. I never saw her again.

Ten years later, I received correspondence from her. She had contracted pneumonia and knew she was dying. She revealed giving birth to our son and told me where he was, yet begged me not to seek him out. She told me everything she could about him."

"You were never curious enough to seek him out?"

"Many a times the notion crossed my mind, however, I honored her wishes and stayed away. I loved her. I still am in love with her. I would have done anything for her."

"So—a month ago Angelique discovered this."

"I have never directly revealed this secret to her, though she is now aware of him."

"How did she find this out?"

"Genevieve."

"Genevieve? You told this to her?"

"No. I never spoke a word to her of this. I never needed to."

"I continue to fail in understanding."

"A month ago, after a heated argument with my wife, I drank way more than I should have and allowed my mind to wander to thoughts I had kept well-hidden for years, especially from Genevieve. You see, my friend, Genevieve has a gift—for reading minds."

"And so—."

"I was thinking of my son," Peter interrupted, "and exposed this secret to her. *Genevieve,* such a vile woman. She always wears that black hooded cape—as if she is the daughter of the Grim Reaper. I had known for quite some time she was adept in reading minds, having learned of this five years ago when returning from Martinique with her and my wife."

"How did you discover this?"

"Angelique's one request before our return to England was that I allow her to bring back her lady in waiting, Genevieve. The very day of our departure, I was approached by an elderly cleric, warning me that Genevieve was a priestess of the occult and that Angelique was her disciple. I scoffed at such nonsense until our ship neared the Canary Islands, when I discovered what a dreadful fool I was. I was strolling alone on deck one night when I noticed a woman who reminded me of Beatrice, the chambermaid I had fallen in love with years before. I had kept our affair secret from all, yet Genevieve read my mind and told Angelique. I overheard them speaking of this."

"With exception for these two, how were you able to shield your thoughts from Genevieve?"

A wicked grin adorned Peter's face as he confessed, "When near her—I constantly thought of vile and sadistic ways to murder and dismember her body. She was most unnerved by the evil lengths I imagined in resolving to kill her. "

Remaining silent, Benjamin mulled over everything Peter had told him. A notion then stuck him regarding Peter's son. "Heathcliff, he is *blind*... and has the ability to read minds—similar to Genevieve."

"Yes," Peter responded. "Beatrice told me of his unfortunate blindness from birth and his *peculiar* gift in her correspondence."

Benjamin struggled to stand, his mind reeling with what he knew Peter would ask.

"No," Benjamin insisted. "You ask too much of me. I cannot satisfy such an unimaginable request. Peter, what you intend of me is mutilation… and murder."

"What good will my eyes be to me after my death, rotting away with the rest of my body in a box? I am offering my son the chance to see, as well as a fortune to live comfortably for the remainder of his life. And I am offering you the chance to prove your theory. As for *murder*, we both know I will not be privileged to see another sunrise. I beg for the restoration of my dignity. The pain I suffer when not under the influence of opium is agonizing. I wish to simply close my eyes and succumb to death. Please do not deny me this."

Hearing the chimes of a grandfather clock alert them to the hour of eleven caused the air in Peter's bed chamber to feel all the heavier. Benjamin dried the moisture of his palms on the fabric of his trousers. Swallowing hard, his pulse raced and his heart wedged in his throat, making breathing difficult.

"Benjamin, my dear friend, the time has arrived. You must begin… now. Please, do not challenge me to beg."

Reaching his quaking hand out, Benjamin lightly grasped Peter's hand, holding it as a tear streamed down his cheek. "I will miss you, Peter."

"As I will miss you." Fetching an envelope from his nightstand, Peter held it out to Benjamin. "Read this to my son. All will be explained to you both. Now do what I asked. You will see me again."

I am a murderer and worse, Benjamin thought to himself. Yet when looking into Peter's eyes, he knew he could not deny him this. Taking a deep breath, Benjamin whispered, "Please relax. This should... only take... a... moment." Under his breath, he faintly added, "Please forgive me."

"There is nothing to forgive," Peter uttered, his voice sounding hollow.

Benjamin held a pillow above Peter. He looked away as he lowered it to his friend's face. Pressing hard against it, he watched as Peter's arms lifelessly dropped to his side and listened to his final distressed breaths. Moments later, noticing no movement, he cast the pillow aside and stared at Peter. Not knowing what to expect, his friend's expression held only peace, as if experiencing the pleasure of a splendid dream. Benjamin leaned down and placed a soft kiss to his forehead.

"Rest, my friend." Echoing Peter's words, he added, "You will see me again."

Reaching into a large leather bag he had arrived with, Benjamin pulled out a jar, having clear liquid sloshing inside, and a scalpel. Testing the sharpness of the blade on the tip of his finger, he swallowed hard as he set the blade down and retrieved a unique pair of reading glasses, having one eye covered by magnifying lenses. Placing them on and nervously adjusting them over the bridge of his nose, he again picked up the scalpel. Leaning close to Peter, he touched the blade to his friend's skin and for a minute hesitated. Though proficiently skilled and highly regarded as a doctor and surgeon his hand quaked in the manner of one who had never before picked up a scalpel.

Benjamin inhaled deeply, attempting to cast aside his sorrow and doubt, and committed himself to Peter's final request. Pressing the blade hard against his flesh, blood seeped from the incision. With a white cloth, he wiped this away as he continued his meticulous work. Within a half hour he had extracted Peter's eyes and hid them in the jar within his large bag. He concealed the incisions and wiped away any traces of blood. The remaining piece of evidence, the red-stained cloth, was cast into the fireplace. He stood there watching it burn until unrecognizable.

Collecting his bag, hat, and overcoat, Benjamin stepped out into the dimly lit hallway, closing Peter's door behind him. Through a window furthest from him, he saw flashes of lightning and wind-swept tree branches tapping against the panes. As he descended the staircase, rolling thunderation caused the wood to vibrate. Standing near the main door was the night butler, a bald and rotund man who could have resembled a teapot if his hands found proper placement.

"Will you see to my motorcar?"

He anxiously nodded but glanced with clear concern at Benjamin. Understanding his unspoken question, sighing deeply Benjamin revealed, "I regret to say—that your master is dead." Lying, he added, "Lord Rothschild passed at the stroke of midnight. Preparations will need to be made for his burial. Send someone for the constable and mortician. Have you word from your mistress?"

"Both she and Genevieve are expected to arrive at the weeks end."

"Send word to Lady Rothschild of the death of her husband. I will call upon her as soon as I am able."

The butler rushed away and within minutes Benjamin heard his motorcar pull up outside. Stepping out and walking down the steps, bolts of lightning flashed, shattering the dark stormy sky. Gusts of wind assaulted him as he reached for door handle.

One of the young groundskeeper's got out of the driver's seat and warned, "The storm may worsen. Do be careful, Doctor Hydenberg."

Chapter Two

"That will teach ya," Clive Cobb, the head night orderly barked in Heathcliff's ear. "Do it again—and the street is where ya will be mopping next."

Hearing Clive walk away, Heathcliff released the breath he held in. Panting for a moment, he rested his head against the cold stone wall and closed his eyes. The pain radiating from his jaw and lips matched the intense pace of his heartbeat. Touching moisture dripping down his chin, he thought it might be blood. He fetched a rag from his back pocket and pressed it to his mouth, wincing when touching the fabric to his lips.

Moments later, wondering if the bleeding had stopped, he knelt down, tracing his fingers over the damp floor to find the mop handle. He continued searching for the metal bucket, taking in a deep breath tainted with lye soap corrupting the ever-present stench of human feces. Heathcliff stood up and began mopping the corridor again, hoping to avoid splashing anyone else who might be walking by, a mistake he suffered for.

He hated this ward, populated by those suffering the most evil warped minds within the asylum. Rapists of women and children and indiscriminant murderers who had succumbed to insanity were confined here. Straitjackets constricted their movements yet their terrible thoughts ran rampant and the high pitches of their screams echoed constantly. No matter day or night recollections of their crimes played out in their violently disoriented minds for which Heathcliff had been born with the ability to read.

Many a morning after cleaning these corridors, he would return to his quarters to attempt sleep. The horrific thoughts stolen from the insane, though, haunted his dreams. No more than one or two hours of restless sleep could be found. He would hide his head under his pillow and pray to God to silence their resounding voices and banish the vile thoughts of crimes his peculiar ability regretfully harvested.

At times, he wondered if he too was imprisoned within these walls. At age ten, with his mother having died of pneumonia, his grandfather brought him here to work, leaving him with the promise of returning someday for him. He had read his grandfather's mind and knew that until his mother's hospital debt was paid in full he would be forced to remain here. But after ten years with no word or visit from him, Heathcliff thought he might never see him again.

More times than he could recall, Heathcliff resolved to leave after once reading the mind of the head administrator and learning his mother's debt had been paid. He had been threatened to be tossed out numerous times since for his carelessness. A blind orderly was bound to miss more than a few things. But where would he go if he left? The world was a large unknown for a blind person with no means to navigate such an expanse. Did charity exist outside these walls? Were he to tell people where he had come from, would they welcome or shun him? Was it worth the risk to abandon insanity and blindly forge out amidst those who would prey on his weakness?

A stray draft of air wisped his hair, leading Heathcliff to believe a window in one of the cells had been broken. The echoing thunderation from the storm raging outside caused the hard damp flood under his bare feet to tremble. Storms always offered him respite from the depraved ravings of the insane as their thoughts were lured to the tempest. Though *they* were frightened, he found peace in not having to endure their torturous remembrances of crimes committed. A sigh of relief escaped him as he hoped the storm would last for hours.

***

Benjamin watched a deluge of raindrops pelting against the windshield and blinked a few times when blinded by flashes of lightning. He felt the intensity of the thunderation penetrate to his bones as he arrived at the asylum. Before stepping out, his gaze was drawn to a flickering street lamp, leaving him wondering if it was signaling a warning not to enter. When illuminated by the lightning, the asylum's aged façade appeared austere and ominous.

This is the perfect place for the insane, Benjamin thought. *No one of sound mind would venture the notion to willingly step inside. God help them all.*

As he approached the main entrance, a high-pitched scream sounding out from one of the broken windows startled him. He had visited this place once before and knew more of the same awaited him inside. Further disheartening was the knowledge that not only men and women were confined to this wretched place, but also children. How could youthful minds be damaged to such a point leading to a grim life as this?

Benjamin banished these thoughts when clearing his mind to focus on the task at hand. Approaching the asylum entrance, his arrival alerted a guard standing near the door. Seeing the guard unlock the door, he anticipated his question.

"What is your business here?"

"I am Doctor Benjamin Hydenberg. It is imperative I speak to an orderly named Heathcliff Gray."

Allowing Benjamin to enter, the guard ushered him over to a desk near the entrance.

"You will need to wait here until the night administrator returns."

"And who would that be?"

"Doctor Bernard Tolliver," the guard replied. "He and the night nurse are indisposed at the moment, tending to a patient."

Frustrated by this, before Benjamin could beg the guard's assistance to bend the rules in assisting him to find Heathcliff Gray, the unimaginable sight of a young pregnant woman left him momentarily speechless. Wandering barefoot and wearing a simple dingy white frock, she aimlessly meandered while twirling strands of her long brown hair. Her eyes appeared glazed as they shifted, though not seeming to focus. A nurse wearing a white uniform approached the desk, drawing his attention away from the young woman.

Addressing the guard, she said, "Malcolm, please return Maggie to her cell—and make certain the door is locked."

"Yes, ma'am."

She turned her attention to Benjamin. "I am Agatha Dunham, head night nurse. May I assist you?"

"Yes," Benjamin answered. "I am Doctor Benjamin Hydenberg. I am in desperate need to speak to one of your night orderlies, a young man named Heathcliff Gray."

"I believe I saw him only a short while ago mopping the north corridor," she revealed. "May I ask why you wish to speak to him?"

"It is a private matter. I do not wish to be abrupt, but it is urgent I speak with him."

"Of course. Follow me."

The dim overhead lights flickered and then turned off from an apparent power loss. Fetching a candle and match from a pocket on her skirt, when lighting the wick she revealed, "This is a normal occurrence during storms."

The candle's light rendered fluid shadows upon the walls as they walked down the east corridor, careful to maneuver around a gurney and two chairs.

Wearily glancing to his left, through an open doorway Benjamin saw electro shock apparatuses. Noticing his attention to this, Agatha remarked, "Some consider the use of that therapy as being barbaric. I assure you, Doctor, all attempts are made to be as humane as possible in the treatment of our patients here."

Saying nothing to this out of respect, though in disagreement of such practices, Benjamin's thoughts returned to the young pregnant woman. "How is that woman pregnant? I should think the male and female patients would be kept separate from one another."

"They are."

"Did she recently arrive in such condition?"

"No." Glancing over to him she wondered, "Why such interest in her?"

Shrugging his shoulders, Benjamin responded, "Curiosity is an innate human flaw. Forgive me."

"In truth, the circumstances regarding her pregnancy are inexplicable." Agatha revealed. Talking under her breath, she added, "We have no idea which of the male patients is the father."

"As a matter of conjecture, could the father instead be—a member of the staff?"

"There has been speculation of this, yet our staff has been with us for many years and is greatly trusted. There have been no instances of this type of behavior in the past."

"How long has she been confined here?"

"Two years."

"Under what circumstance?"

"The murder of her parents. She was found incoherent, sitting next to her mother and father's gruesomely stabbed bodies. She was holding a blood-covered knife."

"I see," Benjamin uttered. Thinking for a moment, he continued, "And what will happen to her child when born?"

"Should it survive delivery... it... will be... put to death," Agatha struggled to answer.

Stopping dead in his tracks, horrified by her response, Benjamin stammered to ask, "*Why?*"

Agatha shifted her weight, clearly distressed by her own words. "It is believed that a child born to parents suffering insanity—will inherit this from both, placing the general populous at risk when older."

"What proof is there of this?" Benjamin demanded.

"I am… simply… conveying—what has been instructed to me."

Exhaling in frustration, Benjamin uttered, "So an innocent child is to die based on speculation that he or she will grow up only to succumb to insanity."

Agatha swallowed hard and appearing ashamed answered, "Yes."

Continuing in silence down the corridor, she pointed left.

"There down at the far end in Heathcliff Gray."

Saying nothing else, she turned around and walked to the front entrance, not once looking back.

***

With the storm's incessant thunderation growing muted, Heathcliff's ears captured the asylum's dreadfully normal night sounds. The wailing from a patient in the distance competed with vile utterances of obscenities and pitiful sobbing. The thoughts of one male patient complimented Heathcliff for his sandy-blond hair before disgusting him with notions of depraved acts the patient wished to force on him.

Attempting to block these thoughts, Heathcliff focused on his mop and bucket until another's thought corrupted his mind. Someone was repeatedly thinking his name.

The urgency this man expressed in needing to find him unnerved Heathcliff. Knowing none of the patients knew him by name, his curiosity over this turned to fear as this man's other thoughts were revealed. Thoughts of murder and mutilation frightened him. Blood, so much blood, and dead eyes staring at him caused Heathcliff to drop his mop and stumble over his bucket. Hearing footsteps rapidly approaching him, overwhelmed by rampant panic he staggered away, reaching his hands out to feel the cold corridor walls as he tried to escape.

Colliding with someone, Heathcliff heard the ear-splitting clatter of metal on the floor and smelled the overpowering stench of urine.

He shuddered when hearing Clive bellow, "I'll kill ya where you stand!"

Grabbed by his collar, he quaked in fear as Clive dragged him away. Having his face bashed several times by a fist, the throbbing on his head matched the rate of his pulse and beating of his heart. He gasped from a tight choke-hold and winced as his left arm was pinned behind his back.

Slammed hard against a tile wall, he heard running water before his head was forced down. He struggled and tried kicking to break free from Clive but failed. The muscles of his body tightened when his face was pressed into near-freezing water. Expelling his held breath, he felt the air bubbles tingle against his cheeks.

Unable to stop his peculiar gift, Heathcliff read Clive's thoughts, and grew nauseous when he realized that Clive was thinking of rape. He had held a young woman like this before when abusing her, a patient here at the asylum.

Pulled by his hair, Clive allowed Heathcliff's face to emerge from the water, for a moment breaking the connection of their minds. Stealing a deep breath, his face was then forced back into the full washbasin, the splash soaking his shirt and his body shuddering with chills.

Spent of energy from trying to free himself, Heathcliff believed he was moments from dying, knowing this was Clive's intention. Unable to hold his breath longer, he released his last breath with the sharpness of his mind gone. Lightheaded, he relaxed his muscles. Before passing out, his final thought was of a man saying his name.

Chapter Three

Never before having committed an act of violence, Benjamin staggered back, heaving for air as he stared at the bodies lying on the floor of the lavatory. He cast down the broken mop handle he used to strike the male orderly holding the other's head within the water overflowing the wash basin.

Still panting, Benjamin knelt down on the wet floor and attempted to revive Heathcliff. Resting his hands against the young man's chest, he vigorously thrust down. In less than a minute's time water began spewing from Heathcliff's mouth and nose. Rolling him to the side Benjamin backed off as Peter's son coughed out more water. He fought to breath, appearing incoherent and confused.

Benjamin stood and tugged Heathcliff up, draping his arm across his shoulders. Leading him out of the lavatory, he stopped when seeing the young pregnant woman standing there watching.

Knowing the fate of her unborn child, Benjamin extended his hand to her and urged, "Come on, Love. Let me take you somewhere safe."

With no hesitation she approached him, running her fingers the length of his hand. Lightly grasping her fingers, he smiled and motioned with his head for her to follow him to a side door. Yet as they approached he realized he lacked the key to unlock it.

Believing the other orderly might have this, Benjamin carefully rested Heathcliff down on the floor and whispered to Maggie, "Stay here with my friend, Love. I will be right back."

Benjamin rushed to the lavatory, finding the other orderly still unconscious on the wet floor. Searching his pockets, he found a set of keys in the last and quickly returned to Heathcliff and Maggie. After trying several keys, he found success with the second to last one and unlocked the door.

The thunderation and bolts of lightning had grown with intensity. Sheets of wind-driven rain blinded him. Knowing his motor car was parked in front of the asylum, he released a breath of frustration when leading Heathcliff and Maggie out into the stormy night.

Blasted, can my luck get any worse tonight? He thought.

Drenched and freezing by the time they reached his motorcar, Benjamin wearily glanced toward the asylum's front entrance, hoping the guard was not looking outside. He opened the door and eased Heathcliff inside the back seat and motioned for Maggie to get in also. Again offering no hesitation, she complied. Once behind the wheel, he started the engine and slowly drove off, again hoping to slip away unnoticed.

The heavy rainfall thwarted his desire to drive fast. Though there was hardly any traffic at this time of night, fallen branches wrenched from trees by powerful gusts littered several streets. The incessant flashes of lightning heightened his tension as he gripped the steering wheel tighter.

Within an hour, as the storm began to subside, Benjamin pulled his motorcar up to the front of a corner three-story townhome on the city's north side. He led Maggie away from the motorcar first, helping her up the rain-slicked stone stairs to the front door. When stepping inside, his housekeeper quickly approached from the kitchen.

Clearly startled by seeing who was with him, Benjamin halted any questions from her and urged, "Minerva, please take this young woman up to one of the guest rooms and make her as comfortable as possible. Please do not leave her side. I will explain all in the morning."

"Yes, Doctor Hydenberg." Attending to the young woman, she remarked, "Poor dear, why you're simply soaked to the bone. We'll find ya some dry clothes and a warm bed to slip in." Leading her up the steps, Minerva cautioned, "Now watch your step. A lady in your delicate condition must take care."

Once they were out of sight, Benjamin rushed outside to his motorcar and assisted Heathcliff into the house. Rather than also taking him upstairs, instead Benjamin held him up, mostly dragging him through the kitchen and carefully down a flight of stairs to an underground study. He helped him over to a long table, brushing papers and textbooks off onto the floor as he assisted Heathcliff in lying down. Leaving for a few minutes, when he returned with his bag, he set it on a desk near the table.

Benjamin checked Heathcliff's pulse and placed a stethoscope on his chest to listen to his heartbeat. Incoherently murmuring and moving slightly, Benjamin felt relief in noticing both. Yet the time for what needed to be done was rapidly dwindling away.

Benjamin removed Heathcliff's soaked clothes and covered him to his shoulders with blankets. Stoking the low flames in the fireplace, soon the fire reignited and bathed the room with warmth.

From his bag, Benjamin fetched his special reading glasses and the jar containing Peter's eyes. For a moment he looked at them and then at Heathcliff.

Doubt filled him as he whispered, "Peter, this may not work, all a fool's errand."

Nonetheless, he retrieved a scalpel and gauze and inhaled deeply as he attempted to summon his courage. As a skilled doctor and surgeon, he had performed numerous operations with great success. Yet none of his previous patients were the son of his now deceased best friend. This time emotional attachment clouded his confidence.

Onto a white cloth he poured a liberal amount of a clear liquid meant for Heathcliff to breathe in. This would enable him to sleep for hours and not feel the incisions or operation being performed on him.

"Dear God, I pray you not see me as a monster for what I am about to do," he mumbled as tested the sharpness of the blade while Heathcliff breathed in the anesthesia. When certain he had fallen into the deepest sleep, Benjamin whispered, "I beg you to forgive me for what I have been asked to do. Should this fail, I vow to spend the remainder of my life atoning to you for this sin."

Prying open Heathcliff's right eye, Benjamin was startled by the color blue he found staring back at him. Heathcliff indeed had inherited his father's eyes; such was the striking resemblance to Peter's. Nervously adjusting his glasses on the bridge of his nose, Benjamin swallowed deep when pressing the scalpel's blade to Heathcliff's eye. He silently willed his hand to stop trembling.

"God help me," he mumbled as he made a small incision.

***

An hour before dawn Angelique entered her Paris candle-lit hotel room. She was not alone. From behind her, adorning her slender neck with sensual kisses, an impeccably dressed dark-haired man groped her body when wrapping his arms around her. The sensation of his mustache left goosebumps covering her flesh; his hot wine-fragranced exhales driving her to rapturous madness.

Turning toward him, she placed a finger to his lips. His tongue traced up its length and devoured it, suckling it in ecstasy. With her other hand she unbuttoned his black tuxedo jacket and then his crisp white linen shirt, exposing his attractive chest and torso. She roamed her fingers through the dark hair covering his pecs and then lowered her hand to his belt. Removing her finger from his mouth, she used both hands to unfasten and removed it. Stepping back from him, Angelique watched as he shed his jacket and shirt, devilishly grinning at her as she draped his belt around her neck.

He stepped closer to her and lavished her neck and bare shoulders with scorching kisses, leaving her feeling lightheaded. Yet she pulled herself from the brink of being lost to her carnal urges. Wandering around him, delighting in caressing his impressively muscled frame, when behind him, she wrapped his belt around his head. Forcing the leather into his mouth she constricted his speaking. She tightened her grip, jerking his head back. Her free hand moved down his heaving chest. Reaching her hand into his trousers, she found his stiff resolve for her. His eyes were large, not with fear, but exuding lust for her.

Angelique forced him forward until a mere inch away from an antique mirror.

Speaking in her native French, she whisperingly commanded, "Gaze upon our reflection. Concentrate your thoughts on how you wish to ravage my naked body. Anoint the mirror with your deep exhales."

She reached over to a table next to the mirror and fetched a candle that had been burning there when they entered her room. Holding it up to the mirror, she watched as his eyes followed the flame. She positioned it against the mirror and held her breath as the flame created a scorched mark upon the surface. In the blink of an eye, she then struck the silver candle holder against the mirror, shattering the glass. From it, a fog-like veil of mist was released. The man emitted muted cries of terror, his eyes spellbound and enlarged as if witnessing a horrific vision only he could see. His body convulsed while he breathed in the mist. Angelique released hold of his belt as he fell limp to the floor. With his lifeless eyes staring at the fractured remnants of the mirror, she knew he was dead when stepping back from him.

Entering through a door from an adjacent room, a stunningly bald black woman approached Angelique. The candlelight caused her deep ebony skin tone to appear ghostly luminous. A wicked grin preceded her spoken French words.

"You did well, my lady."

Kneeling and reaching into the man's pockets, she soon found a large sum of money and handed the currency to Angelique without counting.

"Once more, your gift of seduction has proven valuable," she complimented Angelique.

"As has your tutelage, my dearest Genevieve."

She bowed when hearing her mistress return the compliment.

"We should dispose of his body—as we have with the others. I am certain the Paris police will be stunned in learning of yet another murdered man in their city. I do wonder how they will arrive at the cause of death for these men. Possibly we should stab at least one to uncomplicated their task."

"No, my lady, we cannot corrupt the sanctity of the ritual," Genevieve warned. "To do so—would leave us vulnerable to the darkness."

Stepping over to the shattered pieces of glass, Angelique asked, "Why must we always use an antique mirror? Would not a newer one do?"

"The effect would only frighten, not kill. Antique mirrors retain high concentrations of negative energy, from lifetimes of sorrowful reflections."

Turning her attention to the dead man, Angelique remarked, "I may have been hasty in killing him. He was beyond handsome."

Grinning again, Genevieve moved closer to Angelique and ran her hand lightly through her hair.

"Should your cravings need satisfying, you have but to ask, my lady."

Caressing her cheek, Angelique pressed her lips to Genevieve's, their tongues slithering like twin serpents amidst a forbidden garden.

***

Awakened by the sound of a door closing, Heathcliff held still as he listened to the crackling of what sounded like a fire and smelled a light trace of smoke corrupted by another fragrance that seemed familiar. He couldn't quite guess what the other smell was, but it reminded him of when laboring inside the asylum.

Jumbled thoughts confused his mind about what happened to him. He knew he was no longer at the asylum due to how quiet this place seemed. There were no violent thoughts from the criminally insane terrorizing him. Although relieved by this, the motive for his having been taken away and waking here proved elusive to recall.

Heathcliff realized he was naked under to sheet pulled up to his shoulders. Sitting up, a stinging, burning sensation from his eyes nearly robbed him of his breath. He reached up and felt the bandages wrapped around his head, covering his eyes. The intensity of the throbbing pain he felt matched his pulse and rapid heartbeat. Regardless of this, he did not feel afraid.

Why is this happening to me? I wish I knew where I was taken, he thought. *I am no one of importance. What is the meaning of all this?*

Gripped by a chill, Heathcliff stood up from the table he was lying on and followed his senses of hearing and smell toward the sounds and fragrance of the fire. Feeling warmth flooding over his bare flesh as he approached, an obstacle in his path halted his steps. He reached down and not only felt a chair, but also clothes draped over it. Believing these were his placed there to dry, he felt both his shirt and pants and pulled them on. He stayed by the fire for a few more minutes to warm himself until deciding to investigate his surroundings.

Tracing his fingers along what felt like coarse bricks from around the fireplace, he wondered what type of room he was in. Feeling smooth wood walls, he discovered shelves of books, a table with a lamp, and what he thought might be a hung portrait, though not certain of this. Several times he stopped to listen, attempting to read the thoughts of anyone who might be there with him. But after trying this, with no thoughts captured, he believed he was alone until reaching what felt like a door. He knew someone was leaning against it on the other side, sensing the presence of a man. He could not, however, channel this man's thoughts. There were simply too many running through his mind. On notion, however, was certain. The man felt remorseful and frightened.

Chapter Four

Benjamin released an anxious exhale with fatigue competing against the overwhelming concern gripping him. His legs felt more leaden with each step he climbed and by the time he reached the top step his severe exhaustion forced him to rest before reaching for the doorknob. Once inside the kitchen, not even the aroma of freshly brewed coffee could breathe life into him. He trudged on through the dining room to the foyer and was just about to climb the stairs to go to his bedroom when he met his housekeeper at the foot of the steps. Seeing a silver tray in her hands, he guessed she had brought breakfast to Maggie.

"How is she?" he asked, his voice barely more than a whisper.

"Well, I think, the poor dear seems to have been through quite an ordeal—but at least she has a healthy appetite for herself and the young one she carries."

With a slight smile, he nodded his head. The apprehensive expression on her face, though, foretold questions burning her tongue.

"I understand the nature of the questions you have not yet asked," he said to her. "I am much too drained of energy to know where to begin answering them."

"I need only *one* question answered," Minerva responded. "Was the poor dear in danger?"

"Yes, both she and her unborn child."

"Then she will be safe here, *both* of them will. I shall see to it."

"Thank you."

A sudden knocking at the door caused them to exchange worried glances.

"Go on," Benjamin urged, sighing. "I will greet our visitor."

As it turned out, two men were waiting outside. One Benjamin instantly recognized.

"Good morning, Constable Safford."

"Good morning, Doctor Hydenberg. Allow me an introduction. This gentleman with me is Inspector Horace Coberly. May we come in?"

"Of course," Benjamin invited, motioning for them to follow him into the sunlit parlor. "I believe I understand your reason for calling at this hour."

"Yes—and possibly no," Constable Safford confirmed.

Benjamin's brow rose when hearing this.

"I must say, you appear dreadful this morning."

"I have not slept," Benjamin confessed.

"I recall you and Lord Rothschild being friends. His death must weigh heavily upon you."

"It does."

"You have my deepest sympathy. It is with regret I must press you regarding your visit last night at Rothschild Hall. Lord Rothschild's death presents questions needing satisfying answers, formalities and such if you will."

"Ask away."

"The coroner wishes to confirm the reason for his death. He suspects heart failure but is uncertain. Being that you were with him last night, I am hoping you could shed some light on this."

"In all honesty, I am baffled over the reason of his death. When Peter first fell ill a month ago, he called upon me to treat his unknown ailment. I conducted numerous tests and consulted my findings with countless medical texts... but was unable to match his symptoms to known maladies. I would concur with the coroner's assumption—but cannot speculate the cause for his heart to stop beating."

I hope my words sound believable, he thought.

"Why did you not insist he be hospitalized?" Inspector Coberly interjected.

"When I urged him to, Peter and his wife, Lady Rothschild, refused to allow it. They requested I continue treating him in their home. Both being highly private, I believe they sought to keep his illness secret. I was asked discretion when speaking of him away from Rothschild Hall."

"Were you concerned his ailment could be contagious?"

"At first, yet with no signs of his symptoms afflicting his wife or the staff—I dismissed this and focused my attention solely on him, attempting to diagnose his ailment and formulating a proper treatment."

"What was his frame of mind before death?" Constable Safford asked.

"Alert—yet melancholy. He simply wanted to talk—so I sat there quietly and listened.

"What did you talk about?" Inspector Coberly probed further.

"The shortness of his life and regrets he held," Benjamin lied. "He spoke of our friendship… and how much he would miss me. I returned this sentiment. He was like a brother to me."

"I have other questions for you, Doctor Hydenberg," Inspector Coberly stated, clearly shifting their conversation away from Peter. "It was noted that early this morning you visited the Mooreland Asylum for the Criminally Insane. I must ask you... why?"

Emerging from the hallway, all appeared stunned when Heathcliff answered, "I may be able to answer your questions regarding this."

Swallowing hard, Benjamin composed himself as he walked over to Heathcliff.

"Allow me to assist you," Benjamin offered and led him to a sofa.

"And... who are you?" Constable Safford asked.

"My name is Heathcliff Gray."

"The orderly reported missing by the asylum administrator," Inspector Coberly remarked.

"Why was I reported missing? I left of my own free will with Doctor Hydenberg."

Where are you going with this lie, my friend? Benjamin silently wondered to himself.

A notion occurred to him that possibly Heathcliff *could* read his mind in understood both his concern and what he was attempting to hide.

"There are questions surrounding your disappearance from the asylum," Inspector Coberly continued. "There are other questions as well."

"Such as?" Benjamin inquired.

"How are you two acquainted?"

"Doctor Hydenberg knew my mother," Heathcliff enhanced his lie. "For years he has been searching for me."

"That is correct," Benjamin agreed. "I made a promise to his mother that I would look after him—."

"Yet my grandfather had other plans for me," Heathcliff interrupted. "Being that my mother could not pay for the care given to her at the hospital before her death, my grandfather brought me to the Mooreland Asylum to work off my mother's debt. He refused to tell Doctor Hydenberg where he had taken me."

"We were barely on speaking terms at the time," Benjamin added. "Heathcliff's grandfather cast blame on all doctors for his daughter's untimely death."

"And what of an incident prior to your *departure*—this evening, one directly involving another orderly, Clive Cobb?" Inspector Coberly pressed on.

"One of the patients frightened me," Heathcliff confessed. "He spoke of his vile plans to attack me and his carnal intentions to violate me. I was moving away from him when I collided with Clive Cobb. I am blind since birth. I did not see him. He grew enraged and dragged me into the lavatory where he repeatedly clobbered me in my eyes, cruelly telling me that they might see after he was finished with me. Doctor Hydenberg was kind enough to intervene."

"And—how did you intervene?"

"With the unorthodox use of a mop handle against his skull," Benjamin answered.

"On numerous occasions Clive assaulted and belittled me. More than once I thought he would kill me," Heathcliff interjected.

"He was found unconscious in that lavatory," Inspector Coberly revealed. "He claimed to have been attacked by one of the patients. Clearly someone—is lying."

"That would not be me." Heathcliff unsteadily stood up and unbuttoned his shirt. Peeling it off his shoulders, he turned and revealed his bare back to them. The jaws of all three other men fell when seeing deep welts and bruises marring his back. "Two days ago, Clive beat me. My back muscles sting. Are there visible marks?"

Massaging Heathcliff's shoulder, Benjamin answered. "Yes. I did not know they were there. I will tend to this once the Inspector and Constable leave."

"Thank you."

"Did you report any of this abuse to the administrator?" Constable Safford asked.

"No, sir. Clive threatened to further harm me if I revealed how he terrorized me."

Addressing the inspector and constable, Benjamin noted, "To my knowledge the patients were locked in their cells, except for one, a young woman named Maggie. Seeing her delicate condition as being pregnant, I sincerely doubt she would have been capable in assaulting Clive Cobb."

"Yes, that leads us to another question." Looking away from Heathcliff to Benjamin, Inspector Coberly inquired, "Doctor Hydenberg, did you see this young woman wandering the corridors?"

"Yes, Inspector, I saw her as well as the front entrance guard and the night nurse. The guard was instructed to return her to her cell and lock the door. That was the last I saw of her. I noticed no other patients wandering the corridors I had been led down."

"According to both the night nurse and guard, Maggie is missing—and he did not see either of you leave through the front entrance."

"As I said, Inspector, the guard was instructed to return her to her cell. I imagine he would have been the last to see her. As for when we left, I assisted Heathcliff in leaving through a side entrance."

"I begged him to," Heathcliff added to the lying. "I was frightened."

"And the young woman, Maggie, was nowhere near when you both left?"

"Not that I witnessed, Inspector." Seeing Inspector Coberly suspiciously glance toward the staircase, Benjamin offered, "You are welcome to search my home should you believe she is here. I assure you—she is not."

Watching Heathcliff struggle to sit, Benjamin noticed a passing glance between the inspector and constable, suggesting they had considered this.

He was, however, surprised when Constable Safford said, "Thank you, Doctor Hydenberg. We will take our leave of you both as we will resume our investigation at the asylum." Glancing at Heathcliff, the Constable added, "Clive Cobb's abuse of you will not be ignored. He will be placed under arrest and charged with assault."

"Thank you," Heathcliff responded.

Benjamin watched through the window as Constable Safford and Inspector Coberly left. Pressing his forehead to the windowpane, he asked, "Do they believe Maggie is here?"

"They are at odds over this," Heathcliff answered. "The inspector is convinced she is. The constable has doubts. He trusts you."

"So it is true; you indeed possess the capacity to read minds."

"Yes—but I found it challenging. The overwhelming thoughts corrupting your mind compounded with their rampant suspicions caused difficulty for me to sift through."

"Are you capable of only reading troubled minds?"

"I am not certain. I cannot recall having been in the presence of uncomplicated thoughts, only madness, rage, and cruelty."

I wonder if you are afraid of me. Benjamin thought.

"No… and yes," Heathcliff answered, causing Benjamin to grin slightly.

Benjamin stepped away from the window and approached Heathcliff. "Are you experiencing pain with your eyes?"

"Yes, a sharp stinging sensation causing me chills and lightheadedness and an unsettled stomach."

"There is so much I must confess to you, so much I hope you will understand. I cannot do so now. I am too far beyond exhausted. I imagine you are hungry, yet I would not suggest eating for a few more hours until the pain subsides. Sleep would be best for now. There is a spare bed upstairs where you will be comfortable."

Having led Heathcliff up the staircase to a guest room at the far end of the hallway, after turning down the blanket and sheet, Benjamin helped Heathcliff remove his shirt and rest on the bed.

Tugging the sheet and blanket up to his chest, he stopped when Heathcliff remarked, "I have never known such a quiet place. You might think me foolish for saying this, but I have never felt more frightened than at this moment… and I fear this will only worsen."

"Possibly. I will do all I can, though, to help you. Would you prefer I stay with you until you fall asleep?"

"Please," Heathcliff whispered.

Benjamin rested next to him on the bed. For a moment he stared at windblown tree branch shadows on the wall and listened to chirping birds. A short while later heavy breaths and a light snore alerted him that Heathcliff had fallen asleep. After a few more minutes of hearing this, Benjamin's own eyelids grew too heavy to stay open and he too fell asleep, his light snoring matching Heathcliff's.

Chapter Five

As Angelique stepped out of her Paris hotel bedroom she notice an apprehensive expression cast on Genevieve's face. Distracting her from a trance, she asked, "What troubles you?"

"You received word from Seymour Balfourth."

"My husband's lawyer, for what reason?"

"Peter is dead," Genevieve revealed.

Stunned in hearing this, Angelique uttered, "When?"

"Last night."

"I fail to understand. You claimed the poison will take another five days to kill him. Had you foreseen his early death?"

"No, my lady. The effects of the poison were to be exact. He should not have died so soon."

"What does this mean?"

"That either he took his own life… or he convinced another to assist him with death."

"Who was the last to see him?"

"According to Mister Balfourth, Doctor Hydenberg."

Seeing suspicion growing across Genevieve's expression, Angelique rejected her unspoken thoughts, disputing, "No, Benjamin would never have agreed to assist Peter with his death. The two were so much like brothers. What you are thinking is unfathomable."

"Is it, my lady?" Crossing the room, Genevieve ran her hands through Angelique's hair as her voice lowered. "Your not-so-discreet desire for Doctor Hydenberg veils your own suspicions. You cannot hide these thoughts from me. You wish for more than a simple infatuation with him. When near you, he robs you of your breath the way no other man has. When we are together, your thoughts of me—stray to him."

"I will not deny my attraction to Benjamin," Angelique confessed. "He is unlike any other man I have met. And yes, he is not above my suspicions of assisting with Peter's death. I only wish for this to be no more than a foolish notion."

Tracing her fingers down Angelique's cheek and neck, Genevieve caressed her breast through her nightgown and whispered, "We should return to London. If Doctor Hydenberg truly is innocent, then I will know when reading his thoughts. But… be forewarned, my lady. The sacrifice of our drops of blood added to the mixing of the poison has now been tainted by your husband's unexpected death. Do you recall the omen I spoke of when lacing the wine with the poison?"

Swallowing deep, Angelique answered, "Yes. Should—Peter die—before the poison reached full potency… the Angel of Death will extract his vengeance upon us. We have now been thrust into danger."

Grabbing her book of incantations, Genevieve attempted to reassure her. "I am well-versed in the deception of demons. I possess many spells that may overt their attention, shielding us from death's retribution. In time we may dissuade death's condemnation of us."

"Are you certain you can?"

"Trust me—as you always have." Genevieve lightly pressed her lips to Angelique's cheek and traced her tongue down to her lips. Yet Angelique paid no attention to this, thinking only of Benjamin.

***

The distant piercing echo of a train whistle awakened Benjamin. Sitting up, he glanced to his right, noticing Heathcliff gone from his side. Filled with concern, he bolted out of bed and rushed into the hallway. He released a deep exhale when finding Heathcliff leaning against the doorframe of Maggie's bedroom.

"How are you feeling?" he asked as he approached.

"The stinging and burning sensations from my eyes have not lessened. My lightheadedness, chills, and nausea are, however, gone."

Turning his attention to Maggie, Benjamin watched as she sat by the window, staring out at the late afternoon sky. "Are you able to read her thoughts?" he spoke under his breath.

"Yes," Heathcliff quietly responded. "Her thoughts are of those of a child. I know what you are wondering. Did she murder her parents? No, she is innocent. She found them dead. She never saw who committed the crime.

Clive Cobb was the one who impregnated her, to answer your next question. He raped her. When he attacked me—what he did to her flashed in his mind because of how he had restrained me. He had done the same to her."

"Is she thinking about her unborn child?"

"No. There is no connection of her mind to her unborn child. To her, it does not exist."

"Come on with you," Benjamin urged, resting his hand on Heathcliff's shoulder. "I have some clothes I believe will fit you. You can freshen up before dinner."

***

After a wonderful meal, better than he had eaten in many years, with Doctor Hydenberg's assistance, Heathcliff sat down in a chair in his bedroom. Having been amused by how Minerva doted over him at dinner, fussing to ensure everything was perfect to almost the point of feeding him, his mood now altered to anxious anticipation. He had read some of Doctor Hydenberg's thoughts regarding the removal of the bandages and his concerns for the examination of his eyes. Yet his rampant anxiety corrupted his attention to other thoughts, leaving him with unanswered questions.

"Are you capable of halting your reading of a person's mind?"

"If I concentrate hard enough, I believe so."

"Then I request you not to read my mind and only listen to my words."

"I will try my best."

"Before I begin removing your bandages—some explanations are in order." The tension resonating through Doctor Hydenberg's voice was evident as he continued. "I am not a mad scientist, brazenly performing unnatural surgeries to satisfy my convictions regarding theories I have sought to pursue. I am a surgeon. Although I am educated to perform surgeries of all parts of the human anatomy, my specialty is the human eye with its many functions.

Several years ago I formulated a theory speculating that not *only* the human mind holds the capacity to retain memories, but the human eye as well. All of my colleagues at the time scoffed at such suggestions, branding me the mad scientist I spoke of. My only remaining friend, Lord Rothschild, embraced and encouraged my theory until his *untimely* death."

"He was my father."

"Yes. Undoubtedly—you have read enough of my thoughts to know what I have done."

"What he begged you to do."

"Yes. I—"

"No further explanation is necessary. I understand enough of what occurred—and would rather not dwell further regarding it. This was my father's dying wish, one I will respect. You ended his suffering—and for that you have my gratitude."

Heathcliff felt Doctor Hydenberg's hand massage his shoulder and then felt paper touching his hand.

"What I am presenting to you is a letter written by your father. He requested I read it to you. I understand you cannot read this yourself and will satisfy his wish once I have removed the bandages. I was not privileged to know what he wrote and promise I have not already read his words. Do you have any questions you wish answers to before I do?"

There are many things I fail to understand, Heathcliff thought to himself. *I feel the tension you attempt to hide though the nature of your fear is not defined. But I trust you. All will be made clear soon.* "No," he responded.

"Please keep your eyes closed until I instruct you to open them. And when doing so, open them slowly. The room you are sitting in is dimly lit so as to not overwhelm your eyes with light. Even the most subtle glare might temporarily blind you... should the surgery have been a success."

"You doubt the success of this?"

"To my knowledge, the surgery I performed on you has never been done before... and may never be done again. The intricate array of delicate nerve endings needing reattachment proved a colossal surgical undertaking. I did my very best— yet cannot rule out failure."

Heathcliff swallowed hard as he felt Doctor Hydenberg unfasten and unravel his bandages. With his heartbeat and pulse competing in speed, once free of them he inhaled deeply and opened his eyes a sliver. To his left he noticed a soft glow. His chest heaved for breath as he fully opened his eyes. For a moment all appeared blurry. He blinked in attempt to focus on his surroundings.

"It may take a few minutes for your eyes to adjust from being in the dark. Your father was blessed with perfect vision—so we will know soon if the surgery proved a success."

With his clouded vision clearing, before him was a sight he never imagined seeing.

"Who is that?" Heathcliff breathlessly uttered, though already knowing the answer.

"What you are looking at is your own reflection," Doctor Hydenberg confirmed. "I thought the first thing you should see—should be yourself."

His hands trembled severely as he raised them, touching his hair.

"Sandy blond is the color of your hair."

His fingers traced down to his eyes, still a bit swollen and bruised.

"Your eye color is blue."

Struggling to speak, Heathcliff stammered, "These... are my... father's... eyes."

"Yes."

"Was... did... my own—"

"Yes," Benjamin interrupted. "Your own eyes were a perfect match to his eye color."

Heathcliff shuddered when tears unexpectedly began streaming down his face.

Seeing Doctor Hydenberg's smiling, whiskered face from behind him in the mirror's reflection, he listened to him say, "There is no need to be frightened. Your father bestowed to you a gift far beyond others. He exposed you to a whole new world, one that has been kept hidden from you your entire life."

Heathcliff's chin quivered as he thought of something to say while staring at his face in the mirror.

No, Doctor, there is much too be frightened of, he thought. *I have been stolen from the world I knew and placed amidst the unimaginable. In the world I grew up in—I was surrounded by demons I could not see. Now I have been gifted the ability to see the demons.*

Clearly sensing his internal struggle, Heathcliff watched as Doctor Hydenberg firmly embraced him from behind, his smile never wavering.

"I believe I understand your reaction," Doctor Hydenberg whispered. "Do not be ashamed to confess as much. For a time all in sight may overwhelm you with fear, yet you are not alone. I will be with you as you begin this part of your life's journey—until you find the strength and courage to venture off on your own. Soon you will embrace and cherish that which has been given to you. Until then, my protection of you will not fail."

Swallowing hard to find his voice, Heathcliff asked, "Will you read my father's letter to me?"

"Of course."

Taking the envelope from Heathcliff, Doctor Hydenberg removed and unfolded a white piece of parchment and began reading.

To my son, Heathcliff,

I imagine through your unique ability to read minds you must have known for years that I am your father. I am hoping your beautiful mother thought of me as I never stopped thinking of her. Since the day she left, my life has been cursed for not having the courage to fight for her. It is my hope that once I am dead I will find her in the afterlife and beg to atone for my sin in not being the man I should have been. Then possibly she will love me again.

As for you, my son, by the skilled hands of my dearest friend I have bequeathed to you the ability to see an expansive world I hope you will flourish within. My eyes shall release you from the bondage of the darkness where you were never meant to exist. I regret I am unable to utter these words directly to you. Please forgive me.

My eyes given to you are not only the key to a new world for you. They also possess a clue to assist you in leading the fullest of lives. Without all measures of doubt, I believe Benjamin's theory that not only our minds hold memories, but our eyes as well. For you I have left a treasure for which my eyes were privileged to see and have kept hidden from those who will seek to deny you this. Benjamin will provide an explanation so you will understand.

I ask that you attend my funeral and the reading of my last will and testament. You will be required to stay at Rothschild Hall for both. While there, I wish for you to see all you are able. My inheritance to you

*is there. Should Benjamin's theory hold true,
when you look upon what I have hidden
there for you, my memory of this will flash in
your mind. Take it and leave Rothschild
Hall, never to return.*

*I realize this is unfathomable for me
to write, given we have never been together
as father and son, but I must confess that
were we together I would have loved you
with all my heart. I can only hope that
someday you will think well of me.*

Stay safe,

Father

Heathcliff sat in silence, replaying
his father's written words. "What did he
mean when writing that others will wish to
deny me my inheritance?"

Sighing, Benjamin answered, "This
is the point where what lies ahead of us
becomes precarious."

"How?"

"It is not simply your father's funeral
we will be attending. More so it will be a
gathering of devils."

Chapter Six

After leaving Heathcliff to some time alone in his bedroom, when Benjamin returned he found him studying a seascape painting hung above the fireplace.

"I purchased that from an artist who had spent some time on the Isle of Man," Benjamin remarked. "Minerva and I disagree on that. She believes the scene to be far too somber—yet I find it peaceful."

As impossible as it seemed, the scene, depicting a stone cottage facing the sea, was oddly familiar to him.

"Throughout the years I overheard comments regarding paintings. Until now I had no understanding of what they truly were," Heathcliff said while continuing to study it. Turning his attention to a chair and desk he added, "When I was blind, I would touch objects and furniture, feeling their textures and sizes and constructing images in my mind of each. Now being able to see them I recognize how vastly different some are to what I thought they would be. I imagine this will hold true with everything. There is so much to learn about this new world I am in. I have no idea where to begin."

Benjamin sat down on the edge of the bed. Sighing when looking at Heathcliff he said, "I regret we lack time to ease you into all of this. Tomorrow you will be confronted and undoubtedly overwhelmed when we travel through London to your father's estate outside the city. His body is being interned in a crypt within the Rothschild family mausoleum on the grounds. At that ceremony you will—."

"Meet his wife," Heathcliff interrupted. "Forgive me for reading your thoughts. I still have not mastered the urge not to."

"There is nothing to forgive," Benjamin responded. "In the days ahead, you will require use of this gift."

"Regarding those I will meet?"

"Yes."

"Do you believe Angelique and Genevieve poisoned my father, leading to his death?"

"I suspect so—though the proof of this will most certainly remain elusive."

"But you are not yet convinced of his concerns that Genevieve is an occult priestess?"

"I trusted your father's conviction on many subjects. It was his belief she is as such. She is unusual in appearance and mannerisms. I would entertain caution when near her."

A sudden persistent tapping on the window pane startled them both. Heathcliff wandered over to the window and looked out into the darkness.

"What do you see?" Benjamin asked.

"Nothing more than a patch of the cobblestone road lit from a streetlamp."

As soon as he said this something struck the window with such force, it shattered the glass. Having staggered back in fear, taking a deep breath Heathcliff approached the window, with Benjamin standing behind him. A faint hollow caw from a black crow sounded out as it died on the windowsill, its beady black eye staring at them.

"It must have been lost in the dark and flew into the window," Benjamin offered.

"I do not believe this was accidental," Heathcliff mumbled.

"Why would you say so?"

"Is it natural for a bird to hold a human thought?"

"No," Benjamin answered.

"For a fleeting moment, this one did."

Swallowing deep, Benjamin asked, "What—was it thinking?"

With their eyes locking on each other's, Heathcliff whispered the word, "Kill."

The echoing sounds of flapping wings lured their attention back to the window. Yet when peering outside, they saw nothing.

"*Doctor Hydenberg, Doctor Hydenberg!*" Minerva called out before pounding on the door.

At first startled by the intrusion, Benjamin's pulse raced as he rushed over and opened it, finding her wringing her hands and looking distressed.

"What is it, Minerva?"

"Come quick! Maggie's water broke. I believe the poor dear is in labor!"

Benjamin and Heathcliff followed her to Maggie's room and found her panting for breath and clutching her bed linens and quilt.

"Minerva, bring scissors, towels, and a basin filled with warm water," Benjamin urged. "Heathcliff, take hold of her hand and try comforting her. Encourage her to slow her breathing."

Tugging the bed linens and quilt aside, Benjamin eased her legs apart and began his examination. "It will not be long.

The crown of her infant's head is already visible." As Minerva returned with the water and towels, Benjamin instructed Maggie, "Now, dearest, I need you to push will all your might. Come on now, darling, you can do this."

Minerva dried Maggie's reddened sweating face as she gasped in pain.

"Just one push," Heathcliff quietly urged. "Just one."

Though it appeared she neither heard nor understood what was being said to her, within minutes Maggie's infant slid out with ease from her womb. Benjamin held it and asked, "Heathcliff, I need you to cut the cord. Grab the pair of scissors there."

Heathcliff's hand trembled as he struggled to cut this. When done, Benjamin placed Maggie's child into towels Minerva held and swaddled it.

"Maggie, dearest, you have a son," Benjamin told her over her child's crying. "And a loud one too," he smilingly remarked. Turning to Minerva, he said, "I will need your assistance. Heathcliff, please hold Maggie's son while we care for her."

Minerva eased Maggie's son into his waiting arms. Cradling the child, Heathcliff offered soothing hushed sounds to him, walking with him out into the hallway.

Benjamin sighed deeply while glancing at Maggie. Her blank expression and relaxed breathing offered no impression she understood any of what had happened to her.

"The poor dear," Minerva commented as she assisted Benjamin. "Will she ever be able to care for her precious child?"

"No," Benjamin responded. "I do not believe so."

***

Having wandered downstairs with Maggie's son, Heathcliff stood before the large parlor fireplace, pacing slowly while looked at her son's sleepy face nestled close to him. He smiled when seeing his tiny eyes open a sliver before he yawned.

"Welcome to the world, little man. You and I have something in common. All this is new to us."

Seeing a blanket resting on the edge of a sofa, Heathcliff wandered over to it and wrapped Maggie's son in it. "There, now. That should feel much better."

Carrying him around the room, he whispered, "We cannot keep calling you little man, now can we. So… what would be a proper name for a wee one such as you? Lost to his thoughts for a moment, a name came to mind. "I believe I know the right name for you, *Milo*. Milo was the name of my imaginary friend when I was a boy. He was the only one who would play with me. The other boys were cruel. They would taunt me, calling me names, hitting and pushing me down. But Milo never did that. He was always there when I needed him. I think you need a friend like that now."

Startled when hearing a subtle noise from the entrance hallway, Heathcliff turned to see Doctor Hydenberg standing there watching him.

"Doctor, this is Milo," he introduced Maggie's child to him.

The doctor grinned at them both and said, "I fine name you have there, Milo."

Maggie will never be able to care for him. Heathcliff read the doctor's thoughts. "What will happen to them both?"

Benjamin wandered over to the fireplace and stared at the flames. "Suitable parents will need to be sought for her son once we return from your father's funeral." Sighing, he continued, "As for Maggie, I know of someone who could take her in and care for her."

"Who?"

"In the northern part of the country there is a convent. Sister Agnes of Saint Rose is a dear friend of mine. I will send correspondence to her with regards to Maggie. I am certain she will offer a place for her there. She will be well cared by the nuns."

Minerva interrupted their conversation when entering the parlor. "Maggie has fallen asleep," she informed them. "Allow me to take this young man off both your hands so you can rest before your long day tomorrow."

To Benjamin's surprise, Heathcliff asked, "If you would not object, I wish to keep him with me tonight. I would rather care for him than be distracted with thoughts of what will come tomorrow."

Minerva smiled when hearing this. "Well then, I shall leave him in your capable hands. May I offer anything to either of you?"

"No, Minerva," Benjamin responded and then added, "In the morning see to the repairs of a broken window in Heathcliff's bedroom. A bird shattered it."

"Yes, Doctor."

Looking at Heathcliff, he continued, "You and Milo may sleep in my room tonight."

Heathcliff smiled and nodded his head and then carried Milo upstairs.

***

Once alone, Benjamin stoked the fire and grinned when thinking over Heathcliff's almost instant bond with Maggie's son.

I wonder if Peter would have acted the same way if given the chance to be a real father to his son. Yes, I believe he would have. His life would have been vastly different.

Approaching a desk across the room, Benjamin sat down on a chair and withdrew some parchment from the top drawer. He then wrote a letter. Stopping several times in collecting his thoughts, once satisfied with what he had written he placed the letter in an unsealed envelope. Standing up, he left the letter there and returned to the fireplace.

A subtle knock on the front door pulled Benjamin away from these thoughts. Glancing at the time on a grandfather clock near the fireplace, he failed to imagine who would be calling at one-thirty in the morning. He stepped over to the door and pressed his ear against the painted wood surface. Hearing nothing, a notion occurred to him that the sound was simply the wind or his imagination and that no one was calling at such an hour.

When backing away, he halted as he heard the subtle knock one more. With growing concern he reached for the doorknob yet resisted turning it. But when hearing the sound again, he opened the door and found three dead sparrows.

What is the meaning of this devilry?

Though he had not entirely believed Heathcliff's notion that the crow upstairs had thought the word *kill*, finding these three birds dead on his doorstep proved no coincidence.

Something evil is watching us. But who exactly is this evil being drawn to? How can I offer protection against such a foe?

A black cat stalking across the cobblestone road appeared to have noticed the birds. Believing they would soon become the cat's meal, Benjamin closed and locked the door. It was common knowledge that black cats represented superstitious omens, leading Benjamin to ponder of other such symbols. In the end, however, he could not think of anything within the house that would summon dark entities. Never before had he believed in such nonsense but was now questioning the rigidness of his convictions.

Concerned with what occurred earlier, he climbed the steps and quietly went to his bedroom door. Peering in, he found Heathcliff asleep on his bed. Milo was also asleep, snuggled close to him, pressing his tiny ear to Heathcliff's bare chest.

Relieved in finding them both safe, Benjamin thought about returning to the parlor, but instead entered his bedroom.

I wonder what it would have been like to be a father, basking in the joy of having my own son. Should I have not been such a fool, consumed by endless hours spent with my work I might have experienced this blessing. I regret never finding the time for such a moment as this. Possibly, you, Heathcliff, will in the end be the man both your father and I failed to be. How ironic it is that only now my perfect eyesight sees what was kept blind to me— and how eyes new to you find in an instant what took the wasted lifetimes of your father and I to understand.

He fetched a quilt from the foot of his bed and sat down in a chair near the fireplace. Tugging the quilt up to his shoulders, he rested his head against the back of the chair and watched Heathcliff and Milo until his eyelids felt too heavy to stay open.

Chapter Seven

"How are your eyes, this morning?"

"Much of the stinging and burning sensations have gone away, yet they feel slightly irritated."

"Remarkably—the swelling and bruising are almost gone. In a few more days neither will be noticeable." Changing the subject, Benjamin said, "I believe your father would be highly proud of you in how you have adjusted to all this. And look at how handsome you are today."

"Thank you for the use of this suit," Heathcliff offered as Benjamin assisted him with his black necktie.

"In truth, it is tailored to fit your frame far better than mine. Patting his stomach, Benjamin confessed, "I have added a few too many pounds, due to Minerva's wonderful cooking to further wear this."

"By no means are you heavy," Heathcliff insisted.

"You are much to kind, a trait *not* inherited from your father. He held a distinct penchant for being overly blunt."

Heathcliff viewed his reflection in the mirror, satisfied with how he looked dressed in this grey pinstriped suit and vest over a crisp white linen shirt. He watched as Benjamin checked his own reflection in the mirror. Dressed in a black suit and matching vest and wearing a white shirt and black tie, he stood impressively there next to him.

"While it is customary to wear black to such affairs as funerals, I do not believe anyone will fault you, given how dashing you look," Benjamin continued in compliment.

"I wish I knew what to expect today."

Crookedly grinning, Benjamin remarked, "I have attended far more funerals than others. After a certain point, I grew numb to the ceremony and sorrow which encompass this ritual. I assure you, no one funeral is the same."

Yet this will be different for you, Heathcliff thought as he read Benjamin's mind. *This is more than a simple acquaintance. My father was your friend of many years. I know how heavily this weighs on you and your valiant efforts to ease my distress for this day.*

"How many do you believe will be in attendance?" Heathcliff asked.

"Far too few," Benjamin responded. "Your father's wife, Angelique, was not well received in London society. The fact she was French made little difference. What drove a wedge between her and others was conceit and arrogance on her part. Rumors of her alleged infidelities soon followed, further isolating her and Peter. Your father cared little for the opinions and gossip mongering of others. The fact that they were spurned by society was viewed by him as more a blessing than a curse.

To more directly answer your question, I believe only Angelique, Genevieve, and Peter's lawyer, Seymour Balfourth, will be with us at the service."

Again reading Benjamin's mind, Heathcliff asked, "What of my father's sister, Mercedes?"

"One should hope not," Benjamin replied. "If the devil had a daughter, that bitch would have been Mercedes."

Hearing Milo crying, Heathcliff rushed from the bedroom, bounding down the stairs and found Minerva comforting his distress down in the parlor. "Is he all right?"

"Aw, the little angel just needed a fresh diaper and a spot of milk to fill his belly," she said, easing Heathcliff's concern.

"Rest assured, Milo will be in wonderful care while we are gone,"

Benjamin added when stepping up behind Heathcliff.

Gently stroking Milo's feathery-brown hair, Heathcliff softly kissed him on his head and whispered, "Be a good lad for Minerva," and then reluctantly stepped back.

"He will be just fine," she attempted to ease his concerns.

"We should leave," Benjamin urged. "We do not wish to be late."

Again stoking Milo's hair, Heathcliff felt better when Milo opened his eyes a sliver and yawned.

Stepping outside, Heathcliff's jaw dropped as he pointed in front of him. "What is that?"

"That is my motorcar." The spoked wheels and polished black exterior held Heathcliff dumbfounded. He had heard some speak of such a contraption, yet never fathomed seeing one.

"Is it safe?"

"Well, depending on the driver I believe so. Trust me, I am a skilled with this," Benjamin said with a smile.

When driving through the city, Heathcliff's eyes were glued to the unimaginable things and people he saw.

How did I live in this world and fail to know all this existed? My mother tried explaining all this—but her descriptions offered none of this justice. The buildings are nothing like I ever dreamed they would be. There are so many of them. And the people, men, women, and children, I could not count them if I wanted to. They are so different from one another.

"What is that?" Heathcliff blurted.

Seeing what he was pointing at, Benjamin answered, "That is a horse-drawn carriage."

Before reaching Rothschild Hall, Heathcliff knew that his many questions were on the brink of giving Benjamin a headache. "My apology for being such a nuisance?"

"You are not a nuisance. No apology is necessary," Benjamin responded. "I simply underestimated the amount of questions you would have. I am of fault with that."

"I fear they will be endless."

"Justifiably so, I assure you. You will come to find there are individuals who refrain from asking questions out of fear of being ridiculed for lacking intelligence. In truth, this is a folly. One should always ask questions. Having vast knowledge of the world we live in should be viewed as a benefit, a blessing enabling us to make sound decisions. So... ask away. That is what an intelligent man would do."

When later arriving at Rothschild Hall, Heathcliff was awestruck by its enormity. The towering whitish stone façade and well-manicured gardens suggested this to be the home of a king.

"This is my father's house?"

"For only a few more days," Benjamin confessed, adding, "You father sold this place and used his profit for an inheritance solely meant for you."

"That being?"

"Something only you will find when entering Rothschild Hall. That is, of course, should you obtain it prior to Genevieve reading your mind and laying claim to it before you are able."

"How do I halt her intrusion into my mind?" Before Benjamin could verbally answer, Heathcliff read his thoughts of vile intentions of murder and body-dismemberment. Aghast by what was revealed, he uttered, "*No*! He did not think that."

Benjamin could barely control his amusement over the younger man's horrified reaction. "I never knew your father to lie," he responded. "This was his claim."

"Never would I be able to think such, such—." Benjamin failed to find the word for this.

"I would then suggest you consider drawing your mind's focus to different form of diversion, *possibly*—that of—*infatuation*."

"*Infatuation*?"

Seeing Benjamin staring at him, it was clear he was urging to have his thoughts read.

Since our arrival, you my friend have fallen under the constant gaze of a young woman standing near the mausoleum.

At first hesitant to glance in that direction, when Heathcliff did his heart beat faster and butterflies surged in his stomach. The woman Benjamin had revealed to him continued staring in his direction. Her wavy long dark hair was pulled back from her smooth face, her eyes striking behind spectacles she nervously adjusted on the bridge of her nose. Her lips were shaded a color he was unfamiliar with. As for her dress, while black and simple, the fabric enhanced the curves of her frame.

Why do you watch me so intensely? What have I done to spark your curiosity of me? I am no one of importance—yet your stare suggests otherwise.

"Come along," Benjamin urged.

Seeing an older man approaching the young woman, Benjamin held his hand out to him.

"Mister Balfourth," he greeted.

"Doctor Hydenberg," Mister Balfourth returned the greeting. "We share our sympathy for the untimely loss of Lord Rothschild."

"Indeed." Motioning to Heathcliff, Benjamin offered, "Mister Balfourth, this young man is Heathcliff Gray, Peter's son."

Clearly surprised by this revelation, Mister Balfourth extended his hand to Heathcliff. "I should say it pleasure to meet you, yet under such regrettable circumstances *pleasure* seems most awkward."

Heathcliff nodded his head in understanding. His mind, however, was drawn to the young woman and her provocative notion of him.

I should like to see this man stripped of his clothes, she unabashedly thought.

Feeling flushed with embarrassment, Heathcliff looked away as another introduction was made.

"Gentlemen, this is my daughter, Kristina, "Mister Balfourth offered.

"A pleasure to meet you," Benjamin responded.

"Yes, a pleasure," Heathcliff echoed while not fully looking at her.

"An honor to meet you both," Kristina said, her voice sounding confident yet gentle. "Please accept my deepest sympathy as well."

Heathcliff summoned the courage to fully look at her. Once more reading her thoughts, his nervousness heightened.

He is truly beguiling, dashingly handsome. His eyes hold deep sincerity in their color blue. I could find myself lost in them from dawn until dusk. And his lips, such a craving I have to kiss them. Yet I am certain he would not entertain such thoughts of me, as I am much too plain for one as attractive as him.

A notion crossed his mind to compliment her, but his nerves won an internal struggle, rendering him to silence. Benjamin's question drew his attention away from Kristina.

"Where is Lady Rothschild?"

Clearing his throat, Mister Balfourth answered, "As stipulated in Lord Rothschild's final will and testament, all servants were forbidden attendance to this burial service. Lady Rothschild was infuriated by her husband's demand and most adamant her lady in waiting be allowed to stay and offer comfort to her. When I insisted that the terms of his will be followed to the letter as law requires, she stormed away. I do not believe we will see her until the reading tomorrow morning."

From the corner of his eye, Heathcliff noticed a gathering of birds perched on a nearby wrought-iron fence. Looking at Benjamin he asked, "Are any of those birds similar to the one that struck the bedroom window last night?"

"No," Benjamin answered, his expression turning grave. "The bird last night was a crow. *Those* birds—are ravens."

Both returned their attention to Mister Balfourth when he urged, "We should proceed inside the mausoleum. Bishop Hewlett is waiting."

Before any of them could enter, another motorcar quickly approached and came to an abrupt halt.

"Who is that?" Heathcliff wondered.

Under his breath, Benjamin responded, "A severe tempest, your *dear*— Aunt Mercedes."

Barging out the back door of the motorcar, an unusually thin, lanky woman briskly walked toward them. Wearing a black hooded cape over a matching black dress, Heathcliff stepped back, never imagining a woman to appear such as this.

"*Balfourth, this better be worth my time*!" she bellowed, her warning echoing. "I have not traveled from London for the polite exchange of civilities. I am certain my demon of a brother did not leave me even a pot to piss in and I fail to understand why I must endure even a moment with that vile French prostitute he married."

Stopping dead in her tracks, her stare pierced all of them. Addressing Benjamin, she coldly remarked, "My brother's only friend. If you truly *were* his friend, you would have killed his wife before he died and allowed him the pleasure of spitting on her grave." When turning to Kristina, she lowered her voice and commented, "At the very least, Seymour, your daughter has not inherited your frumpy appearance. She is simple—but I imagine there is a young man of equal simplicity that will make an almost decent husband for her."

Kristina offered no outward reaction to Mercedes's tempered words, though Heathcliff attempted not to think of the obscenities coursing through her mind regarding his aunt.

When glancing at him, her brusque demeanor slightly softened when asking, "And who are you?"

"My name is Heathcliff Gray. Your brother—was my father."

A devilish smirk adorned her expression as she commented, "So... my brother did indeed father a bastard—who has now come to claim his station."

Before Benjamin could object to her remark, Heathcliff casually replied, "My dearest Aunt Mercedes, unwanted devil of a daughter and sister, a spinster spurned of suitors by the frigidness of your boney ass, it is a great pleasure to greet the grand dame of all bitches."

For a moment Mercedes appeared dumbfounded, but then the cackling eruption of her laughter startled all except Heathcliff. Pulling him close to her, she wickedly smiled.

"I believe I have found my kindred spirit," she exclaimed.

Chapter Eight

Benjamin's eyes remained fixed on the casket through the memorial service. Memories of final moments spent with Peter weighed heavily on his thoughts. Only two months prior, they had spent an evening drinking in a local pub as they had done many times in the past. Most of the other patrons were aware of Peter's high social status, yet none seemed to care. No special treatment was allotted to him. They were simply two men sharing tales over a pint or two.

At one point Bishop Hewlett asked if anyone would like to speak but he refrained from doing this. In truth there was much he wished to say, fingers to point at Peter's presumed guilty wife who had not the decency to show her face, and admonishment for Peter's sister.

They should all burn in Hell, he thought. He also succumbed to regret. *I held the privilege of knowing you since our days at Oxford, my friend. Yet your son will never know how well of a father you would have been to him.*

Thinking this, he was not surprised when feeling a hand come to rest on his shoulder, knowing Heathcliff had read his thoughts and was offering him strength.

Thank you, Heathcliff.

When the service was finished Peter's head butler, Reginald, greeted all outside the mausoleum. "Your luggage has been taken to your guest rooms. Tea will be served promptly at four with dinner being served at seven. If you will all follow me, I will lead you to your rooms."

"Will Lady Rothschild be joining us for tea?" Benjamin asked, though already guessing the answer.

"I have been instructed to respond that she will greet all tomorrow morning at the reading of Lord Rothschild's final will and testament."

"Ungrateful bitch," Mercedes uttered under her breath.

Benjamin exchanged a glance with Heathcliff, both content with having this respite from Angelique.

***

Dear Lord, Heathcliff thought when stepping inside Rothschild Hall.

The home's enormity and grandeur paled in comparison to what he expected. Numerous paintings of portraits and landscapes decorated white walls with furniture and objects complimenting each room. Though Benjamin and Seymour seemed unimpressed by this, Kristina's thoughts revealed how also taken she was with all in sight. Her occasional side glance at him silently confessed he too held prominence in her thoughts. More than once he attempted to shield from her notions, feeling flushed with embarrassment in how she wished to delight in ravaging his naked body.

When shown to his room, across the hall from Benjamin's, Heathcliff read his mind and discovered this was his father's room. He closed the door behind him and moved a few steps further in before coming to a halt. Shifting his eyes in each direction he knew where everything was, as if he had been here before. It occurred to him that possibly Benjamin's theory regarding eyes retaining memories might hold true.

"In the top drawer of the bureau I will find my father's neckties," he mumbled.

He stepped over to the bureau and found them exactly how he saw them in his mind. He attempted thinking of different objects or pieces of clothing and enjoyed success in finding each he thought of.

"So… where is this inheritance you have left me?" he whispered.

A knock on his door lured him away from this question. Benjamin stood there in the hallway, shifting his weight and overwhelmed with nervousness.

"Come in," Heathcliff invited.

Before Benjamin could ask, Heathcliff responded, "No. What he wished for me to see is not in here. I should congratulate you, though. Your theory is valid. It is like seeing through another's eyes, which truly I am. I know everything in this room, as if I had grown up here."

"Did you experience this when you first entered Rothschild Hall?"

"I am not certain. I was confronted by so many thoughts. My mind could not separate each." He withheld telling Benjamin of Kristina's carnal cravings out of awkwardness.

"I suggest when you begin your search, you do so alone so not hindered by distractions."

Heathcliff nodded his head in agreement. "Possibly I could slip out after all have retired for the evening."

Spotting Peter's gold and silver chess set, Benjamin offered, "I should teach you how to play chess. Your father and I spent many hours engaged with this."

"No, sir," Heathcliff rejected this with a smile. "I cannot explain how I already know how to play this game and I fear I would hold an unfair advantage were we to play. I have not mastered blocking other's thoughts. I would not wish to be correctly accused of cheating when already knowing your moves."

"I appreciate your integrity."

From the corner of his eye, Heathcliff noticed a shadow move across the wall above his father's bed. "Did you see that?"

"See what?"

"A shadow over there," Heathcliff pointed.

"How could that be?" Benjamin asked. "The light shining through the windows is reflecting in the opposite direction. There should be no shadow over there."

Gripped by a sudden chill, Heathcliff's body trembled with Benjamin noticing this.

"Has it grown cold in here?"

"Yes," Benjamin confirmed as he stepped forward and glanced around.

"Do you believe Rothschild Hall to be haunted?"

"No," Benjamin rejected this. "You father never believed this as well. If there is a spirit now here—it has been drawn in from outside."

"Hostile of peaceful?"

"Considering your father's mistrust of Genevieve and her gift matching yours—I would suspect hostile. We should remain vigilant to any other signs of this."

"Agreed."

A bone-chilling scream sounding from the next room startled them both. Rushing out into the hallway, Heathcliff found Kristina shuddering and out of breath. Pointing into her bedroom, Heathcliff approached her doorway and discovered a large black spider crawling across her white bed linens. Exhaling with relief, he approached her bed and picked up the pillow it had crawled onto. Taking over to the open window, when holding the pillow out, he shook it until the spider fell off and closed the window afterwards.

"Thank you!" she gushed. "Since I was a girl, I have been petrified by spiders."

In truth, I could have killed it myself, he read her thoughts. *I simply wanted the pleasure of your company. There may be another spider tonight I will ask you to remove.*

"I will come to your rescue again, should the need arise," Heathcliff responded.

"Thank you."

As Heathcliff was stepping out of her room, from the corner of his eye he noticed a shadow cross before her mirror and was then startled when a crow landed on her windowsill. It it's beak it held the spider. Looking closer at the bird—it devoured the spider, never taking its beady eye off him.

***

An uncomfortable silence prevailed as all ate dinner in silence. Yet as quiet as they were, their thoughts ran rampant. As observed by Heathcliff, Seymour Balfourth was preoccupied with worry over how Angelique would react when his father's will was read. As for Benjamin, Peter was the constant subject in his mind.

I regret I cannot ease your suffering over the death of my father. Someday I hope you will forgive yourself. You offered him dignity he would have been robbed of had Angelique any say.

Both women, however, were consumed by romantic notions. Though abrasive and abrupt of the exterior, Mercedes silently confessed the unthinkable, her infatuation with Benjamin. For years she had pined for him yet was too ashamed to admit as much, viewing her unattractiveness as a hindrance in attracting his attention. As for Kristina, pheasant proved only one delicacy being served with him being the other. Having never been with a woman before, his education in how to pleasure her was relentless with her descriptive impulses.

Wanting to be free of Kristina's unspoken advances and lighten Benjamin's heavy mood, Heathcliff suggested, "Perhaps we should be dining in the mausoleum with the deceased. Possibly they have a joke or two they wish to share."

Benjamin crookedly grinned when hearing this, followed by Mercedes's wine-induced erupting cackle.

Raising her wine goblet, Mercedes offered, "I propose a toast. To my late brother, from the moment you were born I despised you. Peter, you grew to be the evil spawn I thought you would and eventually shamed our family name by marrying a vile French courtesan. Yet you managed to do one thing right, fathering a handsome son well-gifted in the unapologetic artistry of sarcasm. Give our dear parents hell in heaven."

She gulped her wine, consuming every drop. Though Mister Balfourth and his daughter seemed unsure how to react to this, Heathcliff smiled and drank his water while Benjamin raised his glass to Mercedes and sipped his wine.

After Benjamin, Mercedes, and Mister Balfourth retired to their bedrooms for the evening, Heathcliff wandered from one room to the next. He marveled at the greenery and colors of the plants and flowers in the solarium. The plush red velvet furnishings of the sitting room seemed regal, fit for a king.

When crossing the grand entrance, his attention was drawn to a decorative lamp illuminating a side table. Dangling from its painted glass shade were crystals. Reflecting the light, they acted as prisms, creating an impressive kaleidoscope of colors. He touched a large slender one, marveling at the smooth surface. A realization occurred to him. It was no glass he was touching, but something much harder. The word *diamond* came to mind. Impulsively he snatched this one from the lamp and hid it in his pocket.

He continued wandering through the rooms of the first floor. One in particular drew his curiosity. He entered what he guessed was the library, judging from shelves displaying a multitude of books.

I wish I knew how to read, he thought as he admired the textures of the covers he ran his finger across.

Stopping in front of a fireplace, he felt the warmth of the flames and smelled the fragrance of the burning wood. His eyes, though, were drawn to a painting hung above the mantle. The depicted seascape was similar to the one Benjamin displayed in his home in London. However, in this rendering a stone cottage had been painted. He could not help but smile when looking at this, appreciating the simplicity of its beauty and so much more.

Catching a glimpse of something resting on the mantle under the painting, he picked up a key.

This is very old, he thought while admiring its tarnished condition.

A presence in the library doorway pulled his attention away.

"It was not my intention to disturb you," Kristina remarked as she nervously adjusted her spectacles on the bridge of her nose.

"I was simply wandering around, exploring my father's home," Heathcliff offered.

"Your father had accumulated an impressive collection of novels. Do you read?"

Hoping to hide his embarrassment in not being able to, he replied, "No, I have never been much of a reader."

Stepping close to him, Kristina looked up at the painting and revealed, "I know where that cottage is. I traveled to the

Isle of Man two years ago with my father. Your father invited us for a holiday at that home, such a quaint and charming place."

Glancing again at it, Heathcliff responded, "It is quite beautiful. It exudes serenity some I imagine would find most desirable."

"I find you observation of this refreshing. I believe most men would be driven to boredom by such a place. If I may be so bold, I must confess that I find you most different from other men."

"How so?"

"I have been observing you since you entered Rothschild Hall. I hope this does not distress you, a force of habit I have developed in working with my father."

"I did not realize you held such interest in me," he lied.

"What I find, in my opinion, which sets you apart from other men—is how your eyes pay attention to what you are seeing, appreciating all in sight."

"There is much to appreciate."

Knowing she wanted him to kiss her, Heathcliff swallowed hard as he struggled to contain his nerves. For a moment he awkwardly glanced away, but then looked at her again.

"Would you think me too forward should I confess I would like to kiss you?"

"No," he uttered under her breath.

Leaning to him, her lips faintly touched his. As she pressed further, she wrapped her hand around his head and lured his face to hers for a shared kiss. Left breathless with butterflies surging in his stomach, he swallowed hard, wanting to do this again. The chimes of a grandfather clock startled them, releasing him from the trance he had fallen to. Both awkwardly stood apart.

"Good night, Heathcliff," Kristina mumbled and the turned to leave.

"Good night, Kristina," Heathcliff responded.

She partly turned back to him and smiled before leaving him there alone.

Chapter Nine

"There is something you are not telling me," Angelique commented, clearly noticing Genevieve's distraction. Her expression exuded anxiousness and trepidation, so unlike her.

"A dark restless presence has been drawn here," Genevieve confessed. "It is unlike any I have known before. The hours grow short as its legion gathers. Crows, ravens, and sparrows hold dominion over the grounds. It whispers of an unnatural resurrection."

"How could that be? Peter is dead. We saw this with our own eyes."

"While I cannot offer you an explanation yet, my lady, there remains a part of him that retains life."

"His spirit?"

"No, my lady, this is no essence of his spirit. This is of his flesh."

Thinking of Genevieve's words, Angelique speculated, "Peter's son is here. He is of Peter's flesh and blood. Perhaps he is the resurrection you speak of."

"My vision of this is clouded by the dark presence. I must channel the thoughts of the one you desire." Handing a wine bottle to Angelique, Genevieve continued, "This vintage has been tainted by an elixir of passion. Benjamin must drink only a sip to succumb to its potency. He will fall under the control of the first woman he sees. That will be you. Satisfy your desires for his flesh and then I will read his thoughts. He will be aware of this mind-intrusion yet will lack the ability to resist. Despite all efforts, his secrets will be revealed. Take this to him. Leave it at his door and return. When the clock strikes midnight, he will succumb to your passion."

"What if he chooses not to drink?"

"Fear not. He will drink to silence Peter's voice echoing in his mind. I have foreseen this."

Following Genevieve's instruction, Angelique took the bottle to Benjamin's door and knocked. Quickly returning to her room, she found Genevieve gone. A glance at her clock showed thirty minutes to midnight, causing her to pace the length of her room.

***

Standing before his mirror, Benjamin took stock of his reflection. Having shed his shirt, he frowned when seeing how his abdominal muscles were no longer defined and sculptured as Heathcliff's. With his age now forty, his once muscular frame had not altered that much from his youth. Yet, lacking regular physical activity made him soft.

Hearing a knock at his door, he expected to find Heathcliff standing there. What he instead found was a bottle of wine. Picking it up, he was about to step back into his room when Mercedes opened her door.

"You too?" she commented as she fixed her eyes on his bare chest and raised her brow.

"I beg your pardon?" He could barely utter.

Wandering over to him, she responded, "I doubt if any of us will sleep well tonight." Motioning toward his bottle, she added, "Though—a spot of that might help."

Forcing a slight grin, Benjamin sputtered, "Would... you... care... for... some?"

"Of course! I never pass up a drink offered by a half-naked man. I must confess, though, to never having been *offered* a drink by a half-naked man."

Dumbfounded by the situation he found himself in, motioning for her to sit in the chair close to the fireplace, Benjamin poured them each a glass of wine.

"To your continued health," he toasted, gulping his wine to bolster his courage.

Watching how strangely she looked at him, Benjamin was startled when she tossed her full glass of wine into the fireplace and quickly stood before him.

"For too many years I have kept quiet," she confessed. "I can no longer. Since you first stepped foot in Rothschild Hall—I have secretly desired you."

My ears are deceiving me. Am I hearing this? Benjamin thought. *I only drank one glass of wine. I cannot be drunk yet. I must be suffering a delusion. Yes, that must be it.*

"Please," Mercedes begged. "Say something."

"I… have also felt the same way," he mumbled. *Dear God, what did I just say?*

Before he could react, she thrust herself on him, clinging to his arms and devouring him with unrestrained kisses.

Has the world gone mad? Control yourself!

His mind reeled with disbelief as he returned her kisses and groped her lanky frame.

I recall once yearning to ravage the body of a naked woman. This is vastly different from what I envisioned.

Savagely he tore at the fabric of her nightgown, dragging it down to the floor. Standing naked in front of him, Mercedes trembled with his touch to her sagging minuscule breasts.

It was the wine. I am certain of it. I promise to never drink again, he said to himself as he tasted the flesh of her neck and shoulder.

Freed of his trousers by her trembling hands, he glanced down at his erection and silently noted with shock, *why am I not flaccid? What do you see that I fail to? At the very least—have the decency to share.*

He picked her up and carried her to his bed.

I am possessed by the devil. There is no other explanation. This is my penance for sins committed.

Forced onto his back, she straddled him, guiding his stiff erection into her. With their bodies rocking in motion, he closed his eyes and attempted to imagine someone else pleasuring his body. No matter how hard he tried, though, only Mercedes's face appeared in his thoughts.

As their lovemaking continued, an unfathomable notion corrupted his resistance. Impossible as it seemed, he was actually enjoying being with her.

This is Peter's doing. I am certain of it. Yet—she is—rather skilled with this.

Though it had been a number of years since his last night spent with a woman, Mercedes proved satisfying in every manner.

Rolling her onto her back, Benjamin thrust deeper into her, his chest heaving and his skin damp with perspiration. Her hands roaming over his heated flesh fueled him on. Writhing under him, her cries of ecstasy were soon matched with his. One final thrust buried deep into her, his scorching release robbing them both of breath.

Easing off to her side, she clung to him, kissing his shoulder and chest. His vision grew blurry as he closed his eyes, feeling her snuggling close. Before falling asleep, their lips bound for a passionate kiss.

***

When the clock struck twelve, with Genevieve's nodding encouragement, Angelique snuck out into the hallway, treading lightly down to Benjamin's room.

Knocking softly on his door, she whispered, "Benjamin, it is Angelique. May

I come in?" Hearing no response, she knocked again, slightly louder this time. "Benjamin, Benjamin," she tried calling him.

Frustrated by his lack of response, she knelt down and gazed through the door's keyhole. She first saw the empty wine bottle on the floor next to the fireplace. Shifting her glance, her jaw dropped in shock, seeing him lying naked on his bed with Mercedes's naked body draped over him. Their restful snoring complimented each other's. Infuriated by this, she stood up and stormed back to her bedroom, harshly slapping Genevieve across her face when passing her in the doorway.

***

Jarred awake by a knock at his door, Heathcliff sat up in bed, thinking he had dreamed this. After hearing it again, he got out of bed and pulled on his trousers before opening his door. There stood Kristina, beautifully dressed in a pink nightgown, having a plunging neckline accentuating her breasts.

"I regret bothering you at such an hour. There is something moving in my room."

Reading her frightened thoughts, he knew she was telling the truth.

"Wait here," he urged.

Heathcliff held a finger to his lips as he crept over to her open bedroom door. The low flickering light from the fireplace illuminated only a portion of the room closest to it. Cautiously stepping further in, he noticed the curtains of an open window being disturbed by a breeze. When taking a step in that direction, he halted when hearing the unmistakable flapping of a bird's wings sounding from the direction of the bed. Before he could look that way, four sparrows startled him when flying in through the window. They flew into the fireplace, exploding after impacting against the blackened brick within the grate. The low flames instantly reignited to an inferno, turning their feathers to ash.

Heathcliff's jaw hung low when he noticed a shadow move within the fireplace. At first it resembled the profile of a human head, which then turned to stare at him. Unnerved by this, the sounds of bird's wings once more drew his attention. Glancing over to the four post bed, he shuddered in fear when seeing countless crows and ravens covering the bed linens, cawing and extending their wings as if threatening him.

Feeling his heart choking his throat he took a step back but was halted in leaving when the door closed behind him.

"Did you find anything?" Kristina asked.

Blinking, Heathcliff exhaled deeply as he looked around, finding the room as it was when he first entered. The fire burned low and the curtains moved with a subtle breeze. No traces of birds were anywhere to be seen.

Swallowing hard, he mumbled as he lied, "No. I found nothing."

"May I stay in your room tonight?" she asked. "I am too frightened to be alone."

"Of course," he answered, hiding his nerves of this.

When inside his room, he closed and locked the door. The fear of what he saw in her room faded from his mind when gripped by a new dilemma. Turning to her as she stood by his fireplace, he again noticed how beautiful she looked, causing him to shift his weight nervously. He read her mind, full of thoughts of passion she wished to share with him.

I have never been with a woman before. But as much as I wish for us to be together I cannot do this without you understanding the truth about me, he thought.

Stepping over to her, he lowered his eyes toward the fire, reeling with shame in confessing, "I am not who you may believe I am."

Kristina reached out and touched his hand, entwining her fingers with his.

"I know what your heart desires—yet I am much too unworthy to allow this."

"Why?"

"My aunt was wrong. You are the most beautiful woman I have ever seen. Far beyond that, you possess a brilliant mind. Your father would be lost without you. Kristina, you should be with someone more like you, someone equally brilliant to share your life with. I am merely the bastard son of a dead nobleman, completely insignificant."

"Do not say that," she interrupted.

Keeping his eyes drawn away from looking at her, he argued, "I will not deny the truth. That is what I am and worse. When we were in the library tonight, you asked if I read. I do not—because I *cannot*. I do not know how to read. I am uneducated, never having stepped foot in a school. Before I came here I was meagerly employed as an orderly at an asylum for the criminally insane. I have no skills other than mopping a floor."

Reading her thoughts, though taken aback by his revelation, she responded, "That—is of no matter to me."

Continuing to read her mind, though she desired for this to be true, doubts clouded her conviction.

She attempted to diminish them when responding, "Heathcliff, when I first saw you I was entranced by your handsome features. Never before had I fallen to such infatuation. When talking to you, I grew enamored by your gentleness and spirit and the manner you appreciate all that surrounds you. You have cast a spell over me I do not wish to be free of."

"You deserve so much more than a fantasy. I have nothing to offer you."

"You suffer far too much pressure in discounting your worth. You hold intelligence you fail to credit yourself for. And—I believe there is something else you will not admit."

"That being?"

"That you fear me, that you worry should you surrender your heart—that I will break it."

But you will. Despite your denial your thoughts betray you. Even now the analytical part of your mind questions your attraction to me—which in truth is breaking my heart. I would risk all to allow myself to fall in love with you. Possibly your heart echoes this sentiment. But to love someone, there can be no conflict between your heart and mind. Someday you may come to understand this.

Luring his chin up, Kristina brushed away a tear falling from his eye and attempted a smile.

"One of us is a fool. Possibly it might be me. Perhaps time will tell."

Not wishing to respond to this, Heathcliff whispered, "You can take the bed. I will be comfortable in the chair."

She pressed her hand against his bare chest, above the point of his beating heart, and nodded. Fetching a quilt from the foot of the bed, he sat down in the chair and tugged the quilt up to his chest. Lying down on the bed, Kristina pulled the blankets close to her. Until falling asleep, they stared at each other. He wondered if there was more to say and knew she was thinking the same thing. But neither spoke another word.

Chapter Ten

The light penetrating through the windows was different this morning. Rising from the chair and stretching his stiff muscles, Heathcliff wandered over to the window and looked outside. All in view was pale and lacking vibrancy of color from what looked like grey smoke clinging to the ground.

Fog? he wondered, having heard this word but never seeing this before.

Glancing over at the bed, Kristina was missing. He thought he heard her leave a short while before opening his eyes. Having spurned her romantic notions of him by his confession, he was uncertain how she would react when seeing him at breakfast.

She deserves a man better than me, someone she would no feel ashamed of.

Returning his attention to the view outside, he leaned against the window frame and sighed.

I wish for all of this to be over. I understand why you wanted me to come here, Father. I wish I had known you. Mother seldom spoke of you before her death—but she thought often of you and believed you would have been a good father to me.

After thinking this, thoughts of Milo came to him.

I know Benjamin is planning to give him to a childless couple in London. Before leaving his home, I overheard him say this to Minerva. I hope they cherish him so he will never know what it is like to be without a family... the way I eventually was.

After bathing and dressing, when stepping out into the hallway, Heathcliff halted and watched with dismay as his aunt passionately kissed Benjamin on his cheek before returning to her room. More shocking was that she was only wearing his white linen shirt over her lanky frame and he was bare to the waist. He understood the stern thought Benjamin conveyed to him.

Not one word.

Covering him mouth to shield his smile, Heathcliff nodded his head and made his way downstairs to breakfast.

He was immediately confronted by a chill in the dining room, not in the air but rather from Kristina's cold disposition regarding him.

I was a fool for what I thought. Yes, he is handsome—yet not an intellectual equal. I deserve someone kind and intelligent, someone having a clear vision of his future.

But her resolve to dismiss her infatuation of him easily failed.

Though this man will not be Heathcliff. Most likely he will not set my heart afire and allow romantic notions to consume my every thought as Heathcliff does. No, I cannot allow myself to think this way. I must remain resolute in forging ahead to search for a proper husband of intellect and means. Although for being uneducated, Heathcliff commands a unique type of intelligence, drawing his conclusions from his heart the way most men fail to. No, no, stop it. I cannot, will not, be conflicted over this. He was the one who rejected me. I should curse him. Yes, that is what I should do.

Sitting down across from her, he timidly glanced at her and quietly said, "Good morning, Kristina."

Ignoring an obscenity scorching her tongue, instead she fought for self-control and flatly responded, "Good morning, Mister Gray." She made no effort to look at him.

Swallowing hard as his breakfast was served, Heathcliff read her father's mind, confused over the distracted awkwardness his daughter expressed to him.

Both Benjamin and Mercedes noticed this tension as well when joining them, yet said nothing.

Kristina screamed when a crow suddenly struck the window behind him, shattering the glass. Reginald and a chambermaid rushed over view the damage.

"We have been inexplicably inundated with birds outside, a multitude of crows, ravens, and sparrows. The grounds keeping staff is baffled by how to rid the manner of them. They are creating quite a nuisance," he remarked.

"Has this occurred before?" Benjamin asked.

"Of my thirty years with employment here at Rothschild Hall, I have never been witness to such a gathering of birds," Reginald responded.

With hesitation he pushed the crow's dead carcass out the window and began cleaning up the shards of glass.

The dining room's twin doors abruptly opened and in stepped Angelique, followed by Genevieve. Still turned away toward the window, in his mind

Heathcliff heard Genevieve's words, *Welcome Heathcliff Gray*.

Silently returning her greeting, he offered in thought, *Genevieve, at last we meet*.

Looking toward them, he watched Genevieve's eyes enlarge with shock as she staggered back.

You have your father's eyes. How could that be?

Her mind reeled in astonishment and fear.

"Genevieve, are you all right?" Angelique asked.

"No... my lady. I... need some... air," she struggled to say and quickly left.

"Should I attend to her?" Benjamin asked, standing up.

"No, please sit," Angelique urged. "I am certain she will be fine." She continued, "Good morning, Mister Balfourth." Not one word was said to his daughter or Mercedes. With only a side glance toward him, Angelique forced a greeting. "Welcome, Heathcliff. I had hoped we would meet someday. I regret your father's death as the reason for such occasion."

Liar, he read her mind. *You barely control your hatred of me. I stand in the way of a fortune you believe you deserve. Your conceit tarnishes your undeniable beauty. Everyone in this room understands how my father grew to hate you. Now you will understand the extent of his anger and suffer his revenge.*

After thinking how handsome Heathcliff appeared, a disturbing memory flashed in Angelique's mind, of her and a man standing before a mirror and her lustful thoughts of him corrupted by hate and greed. Heathcliff turned away, attempting to halt the reading of these dark thoughts.

"We can begin the review of Lord Rothschild's last will and testament at your convenience," Mister Balfourth offered.

"Please begin now," Angelique urged, taking her seat at the head of the table, disregarding the formality of having the reading in the parlor or library.

Holding several documents in front of himself, Mister Balfourth read, "I, Lord Peter Rothschild, being of sound mine, do hereby bequeath the entire sum of my estate to my son, Heathcliff Gray."

Her face instantly flushed with rage. Smashing her teacup down on her saucer, Angelique bellowed, "No! I *forbid* my late husband's *bastard son* being named sole heir!"

"*Lady Rothschild*," Mister Balfourth tried to interject.

"No!" she continued her tirade. "Peter was not of sound mind when he came to this decision. He was ill and addicted to opium his final days."

"He was completely sound of mind!" Benjamin vehemently denied her claim. "Yes, he was ill and yes I prescribed the use of opium to alleviate some of his discomfort—but I assure you, his mind was uncorrupted and perfectly capable of rational thought."

Mercedes sat back, smirking, while Mister Balfourth swallowed deep and urged, "Please allow me to continue."

Benjamin and Angelique exchanged glances brimming with hatred.

You were in love with Benjamin when you entered the room, Heathcliff recalled. *Now you wish for him to die. I may never understand the corruptive power greed wields.*

"To my wife, Angelique, I leave—." Again swallowing hard, Mister Balfourth finished, "Nothing."

Grabbing the documents from him, Angelique's eyes seared and scoured the words, clenching the papers tightly, and demanded, "What is the meaning of this? Rothschild Hall has been *sold*? And... and... I am to leave no later than... the day after *tomorrow*?"

"Yes," Mister Balfourth anxiously confirmed.

"*This is outrageous!* Who did Peter sell the manor to? I demand you divulge this."

"The owner wishes to remain anonymous—until you vacate the manor."

"No, you will—tell—me—*now*. I insist." Extending her arms out, she added, "Should I even *consider* leaving, which I will *not*, how would I manage to have all the furnishings and possessions packed and moved so quickly?"

Clearing his throat, Mister Balfourth meekly responded, "In accordance with the terms of both the purchase and your husband's will, you are to leave with… only the clothes on your back."

Heathcliff nearly burst out laughing when Mister Balfourth thought, *on your back, a position you are familiar with according to rampant gossip.*

Angelique's high-pitched scream startled all. Rising from her chair, she tossed it aside and stormed out through the dining room's twin door, slamming them behind her.

Seeing his aunt's devilishly radiating smile, Heathcliff grinned when reading her thoughts.

I hope you will enjoy your new home, my dearest devil of an aunt.

***

Cowering in the corner of her bedroom, Genevieve's eyes rapidly shifted, watchful for unnatural shadows appearing on her walls. On the ceiling space above her bed, a dark silhouette of a tree branch shivered in a breeze disturbing the curtains, causing them to flail like twin ghosts. Her shallow panting rendered her lightheaded. Fear-driven thoughts consumed her. Pressing her hands to her bald head, she wondered if her brain might explode through her skull.

When in the dining room she clearly saw Peter's eyes staring back at her, piercing like knives. But how could that be? It was unnatural for Heathcliff to possess his father's eyes, yet she could not be more certain the eyes looking at her were Peter's. When viewing his dead body upon their return from Paris, his eyelids were closed as they should be. Could the sockets behind them have been hollow? Only by desecrating the crypt could she confirm what she already knew.

Reaching for her book of incantations, Genevieve paged through until finding the poison she had created to kill Peter. Laced with rare herbs, salt, and sacrificial drops of blood from both her and Angelique, the spell she cast was absolute with its requirements. Added to a vintage bottle of wine Peter drank, full potency would be achieved over a month's time until the night of the new moon. In those days leading to his death, he was to experience inexplicable, near-maddening pain no doctor could remedy. Peter greatly suffered, much to their pleasure.

His death prior to the new moon, however, provided a violation of the poison's requirements, exposing them to the vengeance of a demon. Being that Peter was to suffer an unnatural death, depriving the Grim Reaper of his authority, she had conjured a demon to act as a liaison to him, hoping to absolve them of his retribution for their actions. Death would turn a blind eye to their evil on condition the poison succeeded in killing Peter at the proper time. Having died days too early, either by his own hand or with the assistance of another, the Grim Reaper grew enraged and demanded their demon liaison bring their souls to him. To this point, having conjured spells to thwart this, she had kept her and Angelique safe from the demon lurking in the shadows. The intelligence of lesser demons, such as the one in pursuit of them, could be so easily be manipulated and led astray. Yet seeing Peter's eyes staring at her from his son, Genevieve wondered if a dark magic she failed in knowing of had been unleashed by Death.

Frightened when seeing Angelique storm into her room, Genevieve rushed to her and pleaded, "My lady, we must flee this place! There is evil here I cannot conjure a shield to protect us. I beg you."

Distracted from her ramblings, Angelique growlingly muttered, "Peter will pay in hell for what he has done."

Grabbing Genevieve's book of incantations, Angelique pushed her away and began paging through."

"You are not a priestess. My book is forbidden to you." Genevieve protested, attempting to reach for it. "Those pages were never meant for your eyes."

"*Silence!*" Angelique roared, slapping Genevieve. "I will have my revenge."

"Return that to me," Genevieve demanded, struggling to take it from her.

This time Angelique pushed her away with such force, Genevieve was sent sprawling backwards and collided with the wall. Bewildered, she slumped down and watched through blurred vision as Angelique continued searching through her book.

Furious by how she was treated, she intended to stand until hearing Angelique utter under hear breath, "I will kill anyone who stands in my way."

Understanding how unhinged her lady's rage consumed her, Genevieve watched as Angelique teetered on the brink of insanity.

Her madness will see to the death of us both.

Genevieve knew the protections from the demons she conjured would fall should the wrong spell being cast. Inviting another demon's attention and faced with the unknown evil of Peter's eyes, she made the decision to assist Angelique, plotting her escape as part of this endeavor.

"I will offer you my aid in satisfying your thirst for revenge. I know of the spell you need."

Holding out the book to her, Angelique coldly commanded, "Show me."

Chapter Eleven

Having wandered out to the rose garden, Heathcliff sat down on a stone bench and watched from a distance as Mister Balfourth and his daughter drove away. Before leaving, Kristina only nodded her head at him and thought *goodbye Mister Gray.*

"Goodbye, Kristina," he mumbled. *I regret you did not wish to speak to me before you left—but I understand.*

So distracted was he in thinking of her, he did not hear Benjamin approach.

Sitting next to him, Benjamin asked, "How are your eyes today?"

Without looking at him, Heathcliff softly answered, "They are slightly irritated by the glare from the sun."

"And what of the rest of you?"

Heathcliff only shrugged his shoulders in response.

"I know what it is like to suffer a broken heart," Benjamin confessed. "There is no need for me to read your mind in understanding this is what afflicts you. This morning at breakfast, I noticed the discord between you and Kristina. The quietness of your mood also betrays you. I would like to think you could confide in me—should you want to."

Heathcliff glanced down and stared at his hands. "Kristina... wished... to be with me—but I rejected her."

He sensed Benjamin watching him and after a long pause heard him say, "That was not what you truly wished for, was it?"

Swallowing deep, Heathcliff mumbled, "No."

"Why did you reject her?"

"Because—I am not worthy to be with her."

"Why would you believe such nonsense?"

"She is beautiful and brilliant. Her intelligence exceeds her father's. She possesses a spirit and tenacity in seeking what she desires. In comparison, I am an uneducated bastard, frightened of my own shadow. She deserves someone... more like her, someone she would not be ashamed of."

"Do *not—ever* refer to yourself in such terrible light again," Benjamin firmly demanded.

"Before my mother died, she taught me to profess the truth always. When I told Kristina my reason for rejecting her, I read her conflicted thoughts. My lack of education and social station corrupted her opinion of me. To love her and yet know she would feel shame for me would be too heartbreaking to endure. So, I spared her such a dilemma."

"Heathcliff, you are so much more than you allow your mind and heart to believe. When I look at you, I see the strong, handsome, intelligent son I wish I had and am disappointed your father squandered his chance to watch you grow into the fine young man sitting here next to me. Trust me when I say this. You are worthy of the love Kristina offered you. Your love for her would have conquered any doubts she held."

It is too late, Heathcliff thought. *I have lost her.*

Feeling Benjamin comfortingly massage his shoulder, he brushed away the moisture near his eyes and swallowed deep.

Desperate to change the subject, Heathcliff revealed, "I know what else you are thinking. Did I find what my father left me? Yes, I knew the moment I saw it."

"What did he leave you?"

"Do you recall how I was studying a painting hung above the fireplace in my room at your home in London?"

"Yes, the seascape."

"The artist created a second rendering of that seashore, one with a stone cottage and weathered picket fence set on a hill overlooking the rolling waves. This painting is hung above the fireplace in my father's library. That is what my father left me, a stone cottage on a remote shore of the Isle of Man." From his pocket Heathcliff pulled out an ornately crafted and tarnished iron key. "I found this on the mantle just under the painting. When I concentrate my thoughts on this place, vivid images of every room inside appear in my mind, as if I had lived there before."

"I think your father clearly understood what you would most need him to bequeath to you, a quiet home unspoiled by the rampant thoughts of many, a haven of solitude."

Heathcliff grinned, appreciating his father's kindness.

Benjamin stood up, smiled, and urged, "Come on with you. Let us pack our belongings and return to London. You are not to challenge me with our first destination. I will drive you to Seymour's office—where you will speak to Kristina—and confess what a fool you were."

"I assure you; I did not imagine her doubts."

"My friend, no man is an expert when attempting to understand the complexities of a woman's heart and thoughts. A woman possesses the innate capacity to entertain numerous notions at once, at times leaving a man utterly baffled in how to gain understanding of her. And a woman's heart is a secretive place, deeper than the greatest depths of the ocean. You may never understand the motives driving her words and actions. But—should you find your way in penetrating deep into her heart, it is a paradise true to behold—and is always worth the effort in reaching though the journey may be met with frustrations."

Heathcliff attempted an unconvincing grin. "What if she will not speak to me?"

"Then, possibly, the severity of how you torture yourself may lessen—should her doubts of you hold true."

When walking toward the door leading inside, they saw Mercedes leaving.

"I see you are departing for London, as well," Benjamin remarked.

"I wish to spare myself further unfortunate encounters with that heinous bitch lurking in the shadows," she responded in clear reference to Angelique. "The adulterous and roguish men of England should be warned of the vile menace a French whore will soon inflict upon them with her insatiable carnal cravings. Oh, I cannot wait for the gossip mongers to feast on this scandal." Glancing at Heathcliff, she advised, "Never lose your sense of sarcasm, dear boy. I does you credit."

And fully addressing Benjamin, she only smirked and grabbed his ass while passing by on her way to her waiting motorcar.

Under his breath he sternly warned Heathcliff, "*Not one word.*"

***

Standing before the grand staircase and glancing around, Heathcliff asked, "Was my father happy living here?"

"No, neither before nor after marrying Angelique. Your father assumed his role as Lord after his father passed away. It was never his desire, though. He suffered with wanderlust, planning his escape whenever possible. Many a times, I would travel with him to Scotland and Ireland, even as far as Gibraltar. Each time, I saw the regret his eyes conveyed when returning here to this place."

Half-smiling, Heathcliff confessed, "I am happy for him—that he is no longer bound to this place. His spirit is free from here."

"As will we be," Benjamin added as they climbed the stairs.

When approaching their guest room doors, Heathcliff stumbled and braced himself against the wall.

Concerned by this, Benjamin asked, "What is it?"

Appearing slightly dazed, Heathcliff answered, "I feel—feverish—and—winded. I—felt fine—a—moment—ago."

"Let me help you into your room."

His shortness of breath worsened upon reaching the bed. Benjamin helped him sit down and pressed the back of his hand to Heathcliff's forehead.

"Dear God, you are burning up. You did not feel ill when we were in the garden or downstairs?"

Panting, Heathcliff responded, "No."

"We should open your vest and shirt."

Assisting him with this, Benjamin grew more concerned when finding Heathcliff's shirt soaked with perspiration. Easing it off his shoulders, Benjamin's jaw dropped in witnessing steam rising from his skin. It was then he also noticed the chill in the air, startled when seeing his own vaporous exhale. The air here was near freezing.

What the devil is going on here?

Glancing over at the fireplace, he saw charred logs but no flames.

"We should get you to my room," he urged.

He helped Heathcliff stand, expecting to be warmed by the heat radiating from him. Yet he was dumbfounded as his fingertips chilled when touching Heathcliff's skin.

"How could this be?" he mumbled under his breath.

Benjamin touched the doorknob and discovered it locked, something neither of them had done after entering the room. Knowing he did not have the key, for a moment he wondered who had locked the door. But the gap between the door and its frame appeared to answer his question. He realized the door was not in fact locked, but frozen shut by the presence of ice. Several attempts in kicking at the door to break the ice holding it failed, leaving him exhausted and frustrated.

Benjamin pounded on the door, calling, "Reginald! Anyone! We are trapped inside!"

He pressed his ear to a thin layer of frost now covering the door's wood surface. Hearing no one coming, he muttered obscenities under his breath.

As he turned Heathcliff around, his shock intensified, seeing a white glaze of ice covering every wall and surface in the room.

He knew instantly who had conjured this unnatural winter upon them, as well as Heathcliff's scorching fever.

Genevieve, this is your madness. I am certain of it. Blasted! I should have heeded Peter's warnings and been more vigilant to your treachery.

Benjamin led Heathcliff back to his bed, helping him lie down. Within a minute he fell unconscious and his breathing grew shallow.

"Heathcliff, Heathcliff—you must wake up. Stay with me, my boy" Benjamin pleaded.

Embracing himself, running his hands up and down his arms to warm himself, he then rushed to the fireplace and attempted to ignite the wood. With each strike of a match to the kindling, not one spark shone.

"Eternal damnation!" he growled.

Noticing the sunlight beaming through the windows, Benjamin wondered if by opening them warm air from outside could flood in. As he approached the first of two windows, his eyes enlarged like saucers and his heart wedged in his throat when watching the panes glaze over with creeping ice. His body shuddered with chills, his fingertips stinging before turning numbs. In desperation, he grabbed the poker from the fireplace, hoping to smash the glass on the windows. He repeatedly beat at both windows, causing no fractures in any of the panes.

He looked outside, seeing the grounds staff laboring in the garden. Though pounding on the glass until his knuckles ached, the men remained oblivious in seeing or hearing him. A moment later the creeping ice covered the last clear spot, robbing him of further viewing the outside. Attempts to scrape the ice away were futile.

Benjamin returned to Heathcliff's side. The steam rising from Heathcliff's exposed flesh reminded him of being in a stiflingly hot sauna. He fetched the long down quilt off the bed and wrapped it tightly around himself. He then sat down on the bed and pulled Heathcliff to him.

"Stay—w-with—m-me—my—b-boy," he forced out through chattering teeth.

As impossible all this was, when seeing snowflakes falling from the ceiling, his heart sank in wondering if they would both survive this evil.

Chapter Twelve

"Are they dead," Angelique quietly asked.

"No, my lady," Genevieve responded. "The fire and ice ritual is only a means of torture for its victims. To satisfy your thirst for revenge we must follow the ritual I have selected from my book of spells and incantations.

Cowering around the dim illumination from a candelabra set on a wood crate in the attic, Angelique anxiously gazed away into the surrounding pitch blackness. A small mantle clock sat next to them, the motion of its pendulum and droning ticks of its hands maddening her.

"Why must we do this here?"

"There can be no windows, only a single door. No other room here offers the proper setting. The door must remain closed when we begin."

"I demand you explain this all to me," Angelique insisted, her patience threadlike.

"This is a pagan practice not to be ventured lightly with, my lady. I will attempt to summon a demonic being known for granting malevolent wishes. Be forewarned, my lady, for even the slightest indiscretion or violation of this ritual will elicit a fate far worse than death.

At the exact stroke of midnight, I will write my name on this piece of parchment."

"Why *your* name? Angelique interrupted. "Why not write down my name? It is *my* revenge."

"Only a priestess versed in the occult may summon this demon. I will act in your stead in granting this wish. Allow me to continue, my lady. At the exact stroke of midnight, I will write my name on this piece of parchment. I will also add fresh drops of my own blood, using this blade anointed with the venom of a viper and the blood of a raven. A small candle will be lit as the light from this candelabra will be extinguished. The parchment will be placed in front of the closed door and the lit candle will be placed on top of it. I will then knock upon the door thirteen times. All must be done within one minute. When the hands of the clock reach one minute after midnight, the door must be opened and the candle must be extinguished. The door must then be closed once more— as I will have invited the demon into this home."

"What happens once it enters?"

"The candle must be relit and we must leave this room. Great care must be taken in keeping the candle burning. Carry the matches with you. Should the flame go out, only to the count of thirteen do you have to relight it or face the wrath of demon. Failure to relight the candle will result on him conjuring your greatest fear and disemboweling you where you stand."

"What of my wish he will grant?"

"I know what you wish for. You need refrain from speaking it. From one dark room to the next we must wander, concentrating on your wish and watching the candle's flame. When the clock reaches the thirty-third minute after three in the morning, I will speak and the demon will grant the wish asked of him."

"We must wander through this terrible house for over three hours? Why?"

"That is the height of the devil's hour when his power is absolute. The demon may only enter within the single minute after midnight. The following hours are meant to test our resolve for this dark endeavor. The demon will challenge us. We will feel the coldness of his presence and hear his faint vile whispers. We cannot react with fear or rage toward either or we will fail and be shown no mercy."

Noticing the time on the clock as five minutes until midnight, Angelique swallowed hard, feeling her heart constricting her throat.

I will have my revenge on you both, she thought of Benjamin and Heathcliff. *The agony you endure now will pale in comparison to what is coming. Rest well. The gates of Hell will soon open for you both.*

***

"*Heath—cliff*," Benjamin faintly whispered.

The trembling chills his body suffered shook the chair he sat on next to the bed.

I am so very cold and exhausted. Possibly I would sleep if only I could close my eyes. Directing his thoughts to Heathcliff, he continued, *you do not deserve such an end my friend. I hope you are dreaming of a tranquil life in that cottage on the shore. I am told the colors of the ocean and morning skies are sublime to behold.*

Shifting his eyes away from Heathcliff's scorching red body he stared at the abyss of white snow and ice covering all. Whatever sunlight shone through the windows earlier had faded, plunging the room into darkness. He felt certain day had turned to night yet could not confirm the exact time as the clock's pendulum and hands had frozen still. Yet the snow and ice held iridescent quality, causing all to appear bathed in luminous moonlight.

Were I not so cold I might marvel in how breathtaking all this looks.

His jaw quivered, chattering his teeth. Willing his eyes to blink, he thought, *I might be able to sleep now. I hope I can dream.*

His eyes closed as he fell into a deep sleep resembling death.

***

Angelique held her breath, watching the hands of the clock as Genevieve labored to fulfill the requirements of the ritual within one minute. With only a second to spare she completed her task, opening the door and extinguishing the candle. In that instant the air surrounding them grew heavy and cold. The hairs on the back of her neck rose while feeling she was being watched.

Genevieve relit the candle and stood up. "Come, my lady. We must continue with the ritual."

Leading her by the hand, she stared at the flame and thought only of it and her wish for Benjamin and Heathcliff to die.

Descending the staircase from the attic proved hazardous in the dark. The steps were narrow in width and cluttered here and there with unseen items, fabric, boxes, and glassware Angelique thought. She wanted to speak but had not been told she could. Fearful of a violation of the ritual, her words burned her tongue as she fought to stay silent.

Near the base of the attic staircase, a stray breeze disturbed the candle's flame, causing it to dance before being blown out. Stricken with panic, she fumbled to find a match while counting to thirteen. She was able to relight the flame with only one second to spare.

Reaching the upper floor's hallway, she stifled a scream when catching glimpse of her reflection in an ornately decorated antique mirror. She realized the presence next to her was Genevieve, her ebony-colored skin rendering her a shadow in dim light. Also driving her fear were her memories from Paris in how they conjured mirror spirits to inflict death on wealthy French men.

Treading further down the hallway Angelique confronted a second fright when hearing the flapping of wings.

Possibly a bat, she guessed, hoping this was true.

She had seen the crows, ravens, and sparrows circling outside, acting more as vultures waiting for prey to die. Genevieve had explained their presence to her, allies of the other demon lurking in the shadows. The presence of one demon was bad enough to endure. Now with the presence of a second, as well as understanding they had drawn the unwanted attention of the Angel of Death, she felt the strangulation by invisible evil hands with every breath she took.

Earlier she had briefly entertained the notion of finding one of Peter's hunting guns and simply shooting them all. Genevieve had convinced her not to, explaining how difficult if not impossible it would have been to cover up such a crime. Even mere speculation of guilt would have destroyed her chances to retain Peter's wealth.

As they neared the top of the grand staircase, Angelique felt the back hem of her dress being pulled.

Halt your mischief, demon, she admonished the presence in her mind.

Yet it proved far from finished with her as she felt her breasts being fondled and her cheeks being caressed by something coarse to the touch.

Taking a deep breath, she and Genevieve descended the staircase, focusing on the candle's flame and her wish as the pitch-blackness below enveloped them. When arriving at the bottom step the dim light from her candle shown the time on the grandfather clock here in the main entrance. Only ten minutes had passed, disheartening her.

How will I endure over three more hours of time?

Thinking she heard hushed laughter after thinking this, her heart sank deeper as she feared she would fail.

What will happen to us, Genevieve? In her mind she asked, knowing well she would receive no response.

Entering the kitchen, Angelique grew nauseous, disgusted in seeing rats feasting on any morsel of food they could find. The staff had never reported such an infestation, leading her to wonder, *has this happened before? Why was I not told of this? But—perhaps this has never before occurred. They may have followed the demon here like the bats upstairs.*

Both of them left the kitchen, continuing on to the dining room. Angelique held her breath as she saw shimmering spider webs reflecting the candle's flickering light. The tables, chairs, and massive chandelier were layered by thick webs. A rat that had strayed from the kitchen found entrapment in one of the webs and struggled to free itself as countless spiders waited for it to tire.

Is this all real? she wondered.

Again hearing traces of laughter, she thought of herself as being a victim of the demon's vile sense of humor. Genevieve warned they would be tested. But how could one prepare to be frightened and fondled and threatened, though not permitted to react to its malevolence?

***

*T*he height of the Devil's hour

The muscles of Genevieve's legs felt lethargic and strained after hours walking through Rothschild Hall. Channeling her gift for deep meditation, she believed she had honored the requirements of the ritual, having only thought of the candle's flame and the death wish.

Now we arrive at the satisfaction of revenge. The demon is waiting in the shadows, ready to honor its part in this ritual. It can smell its rancid stench of rotting flesh and decay. And the Angel of Death is drawing near for the reaping of souls.

When touching the doorknob to Heathcliff's guest room, though layered in ice, it turned with ease. She pushed the door in and stood in the doorway, her gaze scouring the wintry scene before them. Only having heard of the fire and ice ritual through tutelage when learning the arts of the occult, the power of this far exceeded her expectations. Though she suffered no chills from the blanket of ice and snow covering all, she noticed how Angelique shuddered in the cold.

"How—c-could any—one—s-sur—vive—this?" Angelique forced out.

"The cold is but an illusion, my lady. The ritual manipulates the mind in believing what it sees. In truth it is comfortably warm in here."

Smiling, she watched the snow and ice disappear from her sight, returning the guest room to its normal state. Both Benjamin and Heathcliff lay unconscious, Heathcliff on the bed and Benjamin on the floor. Reading Angelique's thoughts, Genevieve understood that her lady continued suffering this illusion.

"And—and—w-what—of-f—Heath—cliff?"

"I poisoned his breakfast with rare spices and herbs. When ground and combined they afflict one with extreme fever. I made certain to dilute the poison so it would not kill him. He needed to remain alive for the satisfaction of your revenge."

"W-when—w-w-ill—that—b-be?"

Turning to her, Genevieve caressed her cheek and pressed her lips to Angelique's to offer a passionate kiss. "Now, my lady," she whispered and stepped back.

Chapter Thirteen

Angelique's eyes enlarged like saucers, gripped with disbelief in seeing the illusion of ice and snow instantly vanish. The room appeared to her as it always had, nothing seemingly out of place. But this proved false when the low flames in the fireplace grew with intensity. Sparks burst from the grate, landing on a Persian rug to smolder. She could not help but stare at the fire, mesmerized by its twisting motions. The flames reminded her of serpents constricting prey.

Both windows simultaneously blasted open, sending shards of shattered glass into the room, a large piece slicing her cheek. The white curtains flailed in the howling wind, like ghost clinging to the splintered window frames.

What is this madness? she wondered, reeling with fear.

"This is no madness, my lady," she heard Genevieve say.

Angelique continued listening to Genevieve, her voice calm as if possibly not even seeing what her mistress was witnessing or even noticing the blood seeping from the wound on her cheek.

"You were careless, my lady. Your thoughts were only to be of your wish and the candle's flame. Yet they strayed like a wayward lamb. And now you have been lured to slaughter."

Forcibly turning Genevieve toward her, Angelique insisted, "What are you saying? What of my wish? Benjamin and Heathcliff are to die!"

"Only one will be dying, my lady. That will be you."

Breaking free of Angelique's hold, Genevieve stepped back and nodded her head, smirking as if knowing a secret.

Hearing evil laughter bellowing in her ears, Angelique felt her throat being constricted, frightened as unseen hands choked her.

Unable to speak, she thought, *no, this cannot be. No!*

The fabric of her dress tore and shredded. Something raised the hairs on the back of her neck and scorched her flesh. Both her rampant heartbeats and surging pulse competed to cause her lightheadedness to the point of delirium. A burning sensation between her legs left her feeling violated as she doubled over in pain. Yet her body was forced up, holding her too tight to breathe.

The demonic face of a beast appeared before her eyes. Wide eyes brimming with insanity and a vicious smile displaying razor-sharp fangs held her spellbound.

No! she thought as its vile smile widened.

She wished to close her eyes to banish this terror but could not will them to. A viper-like slender tongue slithered out to her cheek, tasting her blood. Sensing the hold on her throat lightening, she screamed her final breath when the beast's claws ripped at her stomach. Her organs and entrails spilled onto the flood. She teetered for a second, her final thought suffering disbelief, before falling to the floor.

***

Genevieve stood back, watching in satisfaction as the beast devoured Angelique's lifeless flesh and bones, leaving no evidence she had ever stood there. The beast vanished from sight, plunging the room back to the wintry illusion from before.

Genevieve's jaw dropped, overwhelmed in feeling the stinging cold.

This is only an illusion, one I summoned as high priestess. I am protected from this spell.

"Unworthy bitch," a deep voice faintly whispered, following with menacing echoing laughter. "As a high priestess," it continued, "You of all should understand the sanctity of the ritual. Your mistress was not the only one in violation of such. How did you know her mind wandered? As the ritual demands, your thoughts should only have been of the wish and the candle's flame. You were no shepherd leading your lamb to slaughter. You, yourself, were a lamb."

Shuddering with fright, nonetheless Genevieve shallowed deep and channeled her courage in demanding, "Who are you? Show yourself!"

"Who are you to make demands of me?"

"I am Genevieve, high priestess of the occult."

"You are a liar and thief, unworthy to utter such claim."

"I have told lies as needed—but I am no thief," she insisted.

Appearing before her, clad in long, flowing dark robes and with its face shielded by a black hood, the Angel of Death extended his arms out and pointed its skeletal hand at her.

"Only I am the master of death," its shallow voice claimed. "You willingly trespassed into my realm to violate my authority. You caused the unnatural death of Peter and sought the same of Angelique. Now my judgement will be pronounced on you, bitch. Welcome to Hell, high priestess."

Flocking in through the shattered windows, a blinding storm of ravens, crows, and sparrows descended upon her, pecking away at her flesh. She screamed and tried shielding herself as each wrenched blood-soaked bit of her skin away. Staggering back, colliding against the door, crows pinned her arms out as ravens attacked her torso. A crown of sparrows jabbed at her skull and eyes, blinding her.

When the last traces of her flesh were cleaned from her skeleton, her bones disintegrated to a white-powdery dust. The Angel of Death inhaled deeply, summoning the last essences of her into him. And when finished, both it and its minions of crows, ravens, and sparrows disappeared.

***

"Where... am... I?" Benjamin incoherently mumbled.

His head throbbed like never before.

If this is what death feels like—then I pray for life.

"Doctor Hydenberg!" he heard Minerva fret. "*Oh*—how I have been hoping you would awaken."

Blinking his eyes, he looked up at a white ceiling as he tried to focus on his surroundings. Turning his head to the right, he saw Minerva sitting next to his bed, her expression anxious.

He swallowed hard and once more asked, "Where am I?"

"A hospital in London," she answered. "Should I call the physician?"

"No, I am merely exhausted. How long have I been here?"

"A week yesterday, sir. Both you and Heathcliff were found passed out in a guest room at Rothschild Hall."

"Heathcliff? How is he?"

"Never better sir. He was released after only two days here. His physician diagnosed him with suffering exhaustion."

"Where is he now?"

Her subtle glance away when hearing him ask this, unnerved him. "Minerva, where is Heathcliff?"

"Well... sir, he returned to your home—but after only one day there—he left. He said you would know where he intended to go."

The Isle of Man, Benjamin thought, happy for him though his heart felt heavy in knowing he was gone. *He is making his escape to the place his father left him. I hope he finds peace there. I will miss you, Heathcliff.*

Benjamin nodded his head in understanding this while not revealing Heathcliff's destination.

Thinking of when he was last with Heathcliff at his home, Benjamin recalled something else.

"What of Maggie and her son?"

"Two nuns from Saint Rose arrived the day before yesterday and escorted Maggie back to the convent with them the same day. They were both most kind and promised a wonderful home and care for her. As for Milo, I followed your instructions and found the perfect home for him. There is no doubt in my mind how loved he will be."

"Thank you, Minerva. What would I do without you?"

She tried smiling though her expression remained troubled. "Sir, while—I hesitate to approach this with you, however, the authorities have many questions regarding what occurred at Rothschild Hall."

"Meaning?"

"Well—Sir, aside from you and Heathcliff being found unconscious, both Lady Rothschild and her lady in waiting—have gone missing. None of the staff saw either leave. Also, none of Lord

Rothschild's motorcars are missing. All the more concerning is that their possessions remain, causing all to appear as if they simply vanished. The authorities are quite vexed by their disappearance, believing they may have been abducted. They are not entirely convinced of this, though, as no demands for ransom have been received. They have already consulted your physician in hopes of interviewing you when you awaken."

"There will be nothing more to tell for my part," Benjamin confessed. "Lady Rothschild stormed away when learning that Peter sold the estate and left his inheritance to someone else. I am certain Peter's lawyer, Mister Balfourth, and his daughter, Kristina, will say the same. We did not see either again."

"Do you recall how you came to be passed out? Heathcliff told me that when being interviewed by the constable, he failed to remember anything of what had happened other than feeling ill and you helping him to his guest room."

Benjamin rested his head on his pillow and sighed.

I doubt he would remember anything else, he thought. *He had fallen unconscious before the snow and ice appeared.*

He heard Minerva say, "Sir", jarring him from his thoughts.

"Yes."

"Are you certain you do not need me to call your physician?"

Benjamin weakly smiled while reaching his hand out to her.

"No. I will be just fine. I promise. As I said before, I am exhausted. I do not know what caused this, though."

***

A Month later

Stepping outside his small stone seaside cottage, Heathcliff inhaled the salty-fragranced air while gazing at the white-capped waves crashing upon the remote shoreline. A somewhat warm robust breeze wisped his hair and unbuttoned black shirt as he observed seabirds defiantly gliding in the greyish-blue northern sky. To each other they heralded what he imagined were greetings. Suspended in updrafts, they appeared bound to the wind.

Passing through a weathered wooden gate, he trod barefoot down a stone path to the beach far below the bluff his cottage sat on. The sand between his toes felt cool, yet comfortable to the touch. Seafoam rolled on shore but then retreated as if the ocean swells were too possessive in offering this to the island and demanded it return. Though mid-morning, the sun remained hidden from view by clouds resembling billowing smoke.

Since arriving at the cottage, the quiet and serenity proved a most welcome reprieve, allowing his mind the tranquility he hoped to find here. A small village, no more than a mile away, provided food and other necessities when needed, yet he vowed not to venture there often. He had not entirely mastered the ability to block the thoughts of others and suffered irritation with his when spending too much time in the company of others.

Looking toward the windblown grasses growing on the bluff's rough terrain, he appreciated the natural unspoiled beauty of this place.

I hope to stay here forever. This place has weathered the hardships of the ages, so clear by how the cliffs are sculpted and shaped. Imagine the stories they could tell if able to speak. Maybe someday when looking back on my life they will wonder the same of me.

As he finished thinking this, thoughts he never believed would again be presented to him flooded his mind. Turning around, his jaw dropped in seeing Kristina standing there. His own mind had been so distracted by peacefulness he failed to recognize her approach until she was just behind him. Standing there barefoot, the hem of her white dress flapped in the gale. Her dark hair blew like a veil captured by the wind, a few strands covering her face. Pushing them aside, through her spectacles she stared at him with so many of her thoughts running rampant.

Willing to halt the impulse to read her mind, he confessed, "I never thought I would see you again."

"The moment my father and I were driving away from the estate, I silently wished for him to stop so I could run back to you. That was what my heart wanted. My thoughts, though, betrayed this, my foolish pride consuming me. But my heart silenced this when a single thought won out over all others. The first moment I saw you—I fell in love with you. Every moment away from you, the ache in my heart grows stronger until I cannot breathe."

"Kristina, you deserve—."

"I deserve—a man who loves me," she interrupted. "I hear this in your tone and see this in your blue eyes. I am not imagining either."

Swallowing deep, his heart wedged in his throat, Heathcliff uttered, "No, you are not."

"Let me love you, *both* of you, if you will have me."

Glancing down, Heathcliff watched Milo's eyes flutter yet stay closed while snuggling to his chest. Overwhelmed with emotion and unable to speak, he nodded his head and she stepped close to him.

Clearly unable to find words to further speak, Kristina tenderly caressed Heathcliff's cheek and kissed him, soft at first and then with more passion.

In her mind she asked, *Will you marry me, Heathcliff Gray?*

He silently responded, *yes*.

***

Though reluctant to leave, Benjamin insisted Minerva enjoy a long overdue holiday at her sister's home in Surrey. Alone for the first time since returning from the hospital, his dark old home seemed much lonelier than it ever had before. Too restless to sleep, he crawled out of bed and pulled on his trousers. Wandering from one room to the next, silence from each sounded deafening to his ears. When descending the stairs and entering the parlor, only the droning of the pendulum and hands of the ticking clock and cracklings of the low burning fire corrupted this silence.

Benjamin reached for a bottle of wine, ignoring two glasses and drinking straight from the bottle.

I should not be drinking, considering the last time I did, he remembered. Watching the flames in the grate he let his thoughts roam, *I wonder how Heathcliff is—and if Kristina found him? She intended to beg me to tell her where he went, but there was no need. I willingly told her. They love each other. I would never attempt to halt such a wonderful thing.*

Thinking more of Heathcliff, Benjamin confessed, *Dear God, how much I miss that boy. In just a few short days, he became the son I wish I had. Oh, I know where he is and may someday go to find him—but for now he and Kristina need their time alone.*

The halting of the clock's pendulum drew his thoughts away from Heathcliff. Stepping over to it, he tapped on the glass and was about to touch the now stilled hands until he heard a tapping on the window close to him. Brushing aside the curtain, he saw nothing out in the darkness except dim light shining down on the cobblestone road at the corner. A windblown branch suddenly slashed against the windowpane, startling him to stagger back.

Taking several deep breaths, he attempted to calm himself until a gentle knock at his front door broke the silence. Unnerved by this late call upon him, he took another swig of wine and swallowed it before stepping out to the entrance. The person knocked one more.

When summoning his courage with the intention to ask who was there, his clock unexpectedly began chiming, leaving him muttering obscenities under his breath while pressing his hand to his bare chest in hopes of easing his pounding heartbeat.

Finishing the last of the wine in a single gulping swig, he wiped his mouth with the back of his hand and reached for the door. He unlocked it and stepped back when it opened without invitation. Standing there in the doorway was a person hidden under a long black hooded cloak.

Instantly he thought, *Dear God, Genevieve.*

Yet what lingered before him proved more unimaginable.

"Good evening, Doctor Hydenberg," a woman's deep voice greeted.

Benjamin's jaw dropped, overwhelmed with dread as the cloak fell to his visitor's feet.

Staring at the empty bottle, he mumbled, "This is your fault."

Standing naked before him, caressing what there were of her breasts, Mercedes smirked and whispered, "Or... should I call you lover?"

About Jeffery Martin Botzenhart

For some writers, their least favorite task is writing about themselves. I agree with them. But since you insist, I live in Ohio, am married and have 3 sons, have a Bachelor's degree in International Relations from Kent State University, and am an avid soccer coach and fan. I'm about as boring as they come...and like it this way. The characters populating my sometimes twisted mind have the real lives. So enjoy my stories and know that the real me is somewhere lost in the pages and pretending to be one of them.

Social Media

Facebook:
www.facebook.com/jefferymartinbotzenhart
writingjourney

Twitter: https://twitter.com/JBotzenhart
@JBotzenhart

If you enjoyed this story, check out these other Solstice Publishing books by Jeffery Martin Botzenhart:

Shallow Hill

A devil's playground

Beneath the crisp white snow crowning the headstones of Shallow Hill, restless spirit voices echo warnings of danger. Brianna's gift of conversing with the dead is tested to its limits when the man she loves falls victim to those suffering minds warped by greed and sadism. In waging battle against these all too human demons to save him, the once hallowed graveyard grounds alters its serenity when tainted by horrors and perversions, offering no escape for some.

https://bookgoodies.com/a/B0792GYBNC

Creature of the Night

Some souls were not meant to lead lives in the sun. They remain hidden within dark realms in fear of being seen and misunderstood. That is Ian's fate after suffering at the hands of a demon blinded by rage and sorrow. Yet there exists a threat in the light, spreading lies driven by fear in warning others to be weary of the unknown prowling the depths of the forest. The unyielding belief in the justification of cruelty in seeking to end that which has been branded as profane proves all consuming. When entering the forest after twilight to pronounce final judgement for those in hiding, the threshold of good versus evil is blurred by the righteous. And thus a question may be asked. Who is the true creature of the night?

https://bookgoodies.com/a/B075ZZMGGN

Harvest Fever

Bullied by classmates and abused by his stepdad, seventeen year old Orrville Fletcher plans to leave his run-down home outside Birchwood Hollow, Tennessee once he turns eighteen. But one night after fighting off his stepdad, his escape from this small remote town in Appalachia is halted by an unimaginable invasion of space aliens, leading him to revelations of an unexpected truth.

https://bookgoodies.com/a/B074JZV44F